A Recipe Called Home

Stephanie Nelson

Threefold Ink

For my grandmothers.

Prologue

2003

Jules dabbed a damp cloth against the fresh splatters of tomato sauce dotting her t-shirt.

"Messy is just a stop on the road to beautiful," her grandmother said with a knowing smile, stirring the pot of sauce as it simmered on the stove—a phrase Jules had heard more times than she could count.

"Yeah, it's messy alright," Jules retorted, trying in vain to blot the stains away.

Wearing her favorite boy band t-shirt to make sauce and meatballs had been a risky move, and Jules knew better. Rosa, on the other hand, always tied on her faded blue apron, worn thin from years in the kitchen.

To Jules, her grandmother was the best cook in the world, though, at ten years old, her experience was limited. Still, anyone lucky enough to sit at Rosa's table agreed. Watching her work was like witnessing a delicate ballet; every stir, every sprinkle of seasoning was a step in a dance she performed with effortless grace.

Jules wondered how many hours her grandma had spent in a kitchen. She'd been cooking since she was old enough to hold a wooden spoon. It was in her blood, just as it was in Jules'.

"Stop fussing and hand me the bowl of meatballs," her grandmother huffed. "It's time to put them in the sauce. Pay attention to how I drop them in. It affects the cook."

Jules passed the bowl while edging closer to the stove, squinting her eyes at the bright summer sun streaming through the windows. The light bathed the small kitchen in that late summer golden glow that tinted childhood memories.

For as long as she could remember, Sunday afternoons meant sauce and pasta at her grandparents' house. In many ways, it was the only real home Jules had ever known. Her mother often dropped her off for days or even weeks at a time, and over the years, it had become routine. Between the constant shuffle of relationships and a string of unstable apartments, Jules understood that her mom, Barb, struggled with the responsibilities of raising a child.

Still, Jules did not mind. Her grandparents welcomed her without hesitation, even converting an unused office into a bedroom just for her. It was nothing fancy, just a futon, an old box TV, and four walls that made her feel safe. It was hers. And that was enough.

After the sauce and meatballs simmered for hours, they finally sat down at the formal dining room table to eat with her grandpa Lou.

With his mouth full, he mumbled, "The best pasta this side of the Atlantic."

Jules snorted. "You always say that."

"That's because it's true," he replied with a grin.

Although they'd eaten her grandma's spaghetti hundreds, maybe even thousands of times, they still savored every bite. The deep red tomato sauce had a perfect balance of acidity and sweetness, and paired with the hand-rolled meatballs and fresh pasta noodles, it felt like a hug on a plate.

Jules knew from a young age that she wanted to be a chef when she grew up. She dreamt of cooking up new dishes in her very own restaurant, not just at home like her grandma.

Some nights before bed, Grandma Rosa would tell Jules stories of her childhood living on the north side of Chicago. She shared memories of their family's restaurant and the pride it brought to her parents. Rosa's father had opened it as a young man, building it into a neighborhood staple and one of the best places in Chicago to get an authentic Sicilian meal that tasted like home.

After dinner, Jules helped her grandpa clear the plates from the table and wash them in the porcelain kitchen sink as he did every night. Rosa cooked; Lou cleaned. It had worked for them for nearly forty years.

Once all the washing had finished and everything was back in its rightful place, Jules joined her grandma in the cozy TV room upstairs to watch Jeopardy, like usual.

Tonight, though, Jules couldn't sit still; energy buzzed through her like an electrical current. Cooking with her grandma had reignited her quest to become a chef, and she needed to know how she could make it happen.

"Do I have to go to college, or can I start after high school?" she asked her grandma before peppering her with a dozen more questions.

Once Jules caught her breath, Grandma Rosa reached across the sofa to hold her hand and said, "You'll find your own way, baby girl. I promise you that."

Chapter 1

September 2023

"Oh, for Christ's sake," Jules said under her breath, looking up at the departure screen near her gate. Her flight from Washington, D.C. to Chicago was delayed. Again. She'd already been at the airport for two hours.

Slinging her large brown leather tote over her shoulder, Jules scanned the area for the closest bar. If she was going to be stuck here, a glass of wine would help while she used the time to catch up on emails.

The airport was packed, especially for a Friday evening. Most of the restaurants were fast-food places with lines so long they'd curled into the walkway. Her eyes trailed down to the end of the terminal, past the hordes of serious-looking business fliers and stressed families, spotting a sports-themed restaurant with a decent-sized bar. She beelined it before other delayed fliers snatched the empty stools.

As she wove through the crowded bar toward the last open seat, her phone chimed. Jules recognized the ringtone. Her boss. She dug through her bag, frantic to find it. Just as her fingers closed around the phone, a burly man barreled past, shoving her aside and dropping heavily onto the barstool she'd been aiming for.

Biting her tongue, she pressed the phone to her ear. "Hi, Becca. Everything ok?" she asked, forcing her voice to sound pleasant.

Her eyes scanned the room again until she spotted an empty table in the corner, dropping her large bag on top of the crumb-sprinkled surface.

"Jules, thank God you picked up. I thought maybe you'd be on the plane already," she said, almost out of breath. "The secretary is having a meltdown. He just read the draft of the speech for the luncheon tomorrow. Says the tone is too playful to match his authentic self. His words, not mine."

Becca was good at multitasking, so Jules knew she was likely also replying to a barrage of emails from Steve Monahan, U.S. Treasury Secretary, while she gave Jules this all too familiar feedback. Becca was his chief of staff and Jules had worked with her as a senior speechwriter for the past three years.

"Did you remind him that the lunch is for the Children's National Hospital and will be attended by sick *children* and their families?" Jules asked.

"Yes, but he says that he needs to be perceived as a serious leader if he's going to get another cabinet appointment." Jules could almost hear Becca's eyes roll as she said it. They both knew his reputation of being a chilly, calculated politician throughout the beltway.

"A little levity and warmth can't hurt," she said. "It's a room full of sick children. I'm still not sure why he was even asked to speak, honestly. Doesn't seem like an obvious fit."

Becca sighed, agreeing with Jules but also reminding her he's the boss and it's his speech.

"Alright, I'll make some tweaks before my flight," Jules responded, resigned.

This was just about how every speech she'd written lately had gone. The secretary waited until the night before every speaking event to review the draft remarks and then demand changes that made little sense. He was a total control freak who expected perfection, like most of the politicians she'd written for. But it was getting harder and harder to take the feedback. Jules craved more creative control over her words, and working for Secretary Monahan felt like running on a hamster wheel. Speech after speech, it never changed.

Jules had been speechwriting since she moved to D.C. the week after graduation for a communications role with a senator she'd interned with. She fell into the profession while on the campaign trail; their only speechwriter had come down with the swine flu, and the team needed someone to write a speech for the very next morning. Ever since, she'd been writing for politicians throughout Washington, and she mostly liked it. Parts of the job fit her well: the solitude of writing and creating, the rush she felt when watching someone deliver the words she wrote. Mostly, though, Jules enjoyed the way it made her feel useful and kept her busy. Not to mention, it was a respectable and sometimes lucrative job.

"Thanks, you're an angel. I hope you get to Chicago soon. And don't worry about a thing while you're gone. Just focus on getting your grandma better. I've got you," Becca said before ending the call.

Jules looked around to flag down the nearest server; she needed that wine.

Ten long minutes later, she sipped stale chardonnay at the dim, sticky table. Begrudgingly, she opened her laptop to start revisions but couldn't keep her mind focused as she worried about her grandma and what it would be like to stay at her house without her grandpa Lou. Grief reared its ugly head once again as she remembered the last time she flew home to attend his funeral with her then-fiancé. It had been a hard trip, one that she had tried desperately to forget.

This time would be different, she consoled herself. For one, she wasn't with Luke anymore, and two, her grandma, who refused to go to an inpatient rehab center after her recent hip replacement, needed her. Spending a month in Riverbend wasn't exactly what she wanted to do, but she owed it to Grandma Rosa. She was the closest family Jules had.

"Right. The speech," Jules said aloud to no one. She needed to focus.

Rereading the draft on her laptop, Jules decided the lines she thought were her best work in the whole thing, the parts that felt most authentic and less political, had to go. They were not what the secretary had in mind, clearly. He wanted something more cookie cutter. More campaign speech, less inspirational words for sick kids.

After slicing and dicing the piece enough to satisfy her boss, she emailed it to Becca, signing off with a heartfelt thank you for taking care of things while she was away.

In a way, Jules admired Becca. She was one of those type-A people who flocked to Washington after graduating from a top-tier school, political science degree in tow. Everything about her said "Professional-Woman-With-Goals-To-Achieve," even her choice of wardrobe, which was always a simple black shift dress. But lately, Jules had wondered if that kind of life, one totally consumed by work and professional success, was what she wanted. Was Becca happy or did she just put on a good front? The questions were never too far from Jules' mind these days.

Two disappointing glasses of wine later, she boarded the plane. Sitting in the aisle seat of her row, a teenage boy wearing a grey hoodie pulled over his headphones looked up at her as she caught the vague smell of weed.

"Excuse me," Jules muttered, hoping he'd get up and let her slide into her window seat. No such luck. He grunted and motioned for her to climb over.

"You've got to be kidding me," she mumbled as she stepped over his legs, making sure to "accidentally" bump him in the head with her large tote bag.

After pushing her bag under the seat in front of her, she sat back, buckled the seatbelt, and rolled the tension out of her tight shoulders. She could finally relax for a few hours.

The flight to O'Hare was just under two hours, where her mom would pick her up. Jules had made the trip a dozen times, often working straight through, but not today. Her mind was stuck in a loop thinking about her career and how this month-long trip might derail her plans, which only made her feel guilty because Grandma Rosa deserved her full attention. There was a lot to process.

Secretary Monahan didn't know yet, but Becca planned to leave at the end of the year to start her own public relations and political advisory firm. She wanted Jules to come with her as the firm's chief communications officer. Logically, it made sense and part of her couldn't help but be excited to step into a leadership role, but every time she thought long enough about it, her belly flipped and turned sour as a fresh pang of anxiety pulsed in her throat. Jules tried to convince herself imposter syndrome was to blame, but it felt much deeper.

Determined to quiet her thoughts, Jules popped in her earbuds to zone out to the newest true crime murder podcast she'd downloaded that morning. Oddly, it always helped her to relax.

A few episodes later, they landed, and she exited the plane as quickly as possible before heading straight to baggage claim to find her ginormous suitcase that weighed about as much as her. Heaving it out to the arrivals curb, she spotted her mom's old

Honda Civic, shocked to see it still running. Barb had acquired it as a parting gift years ago during a nasty break up.

"Hey, you," said Barb as she met Jules on the curb. "Look at your dark hair! Last time I saw you, it was blonde!" She turned Jules around by the shoulders to get a better look.

"Hi, Mom. Nice to see you, too," Jules responded, taking a slow and intentional step back. She'd never been crazy about people touching her hair, let alone crowding her personal space. "I dyed it dark a while ago—it's easier to manage this way. I don't have to go to the salon as much."

In truth, Jules dyed her hair the day she got back from her last trip to Riverbend, after she broke things off with her fiancé, Luke. She wanted to physically match the change she felt inside. It turned out to be a blessing; she spent less money on it now and she liked to think it complemented her sharp features.

After hulling her luggage into the trunk, they pulled away from the airport, taking two wrong turns before finally entering the on-ramp for I-90, going in the right direction. Finally releasing a tense grip on the GPS, they settled into an uncomfortable yet familiar silence.

She didn't know how to talk to her mom and never had. They could talk about Rosa, but then that would lead to a conversation about why Barb couldn't take care of her and Jules already knew this story. It was always the same. Some version of a new guy in her life taking priority over anything else.

Barb was a "go-with-the-flow" kind of person who centered her life around the attention of men. It had been this way for as long as she could remember. Now that Jules was an adult, she'd begun to realize what little self-esteem her mother must have had.

After a few minutes, Barb spoke, "I know what you're thinking. And I'm sorry I can't be there to help. This time is different, though. I promise."

Jules angled her head toward her window to watch the green cornfields zip by without responding. There was nothing to say. All it did was stir up old feelings of being forced to grow up young so she could fill in the gaps her mother left empty. Even at the age of ten, she had woken her mother up every morning to make sure she wasn't late for her shift at the Piggly Wiggly. Jules didn't expect her to change now.

As they drove up to her grandparents' house, she spotted the bright red Volkswagen Beetle in the driveway. Her best friend Winnie was already inside, chatting away with Grandma Rosa. She wondered how long she'd been there, silently cringing. Her grandma thought of Winnie as a "small doses" friend, preferring to spend as little time alone with her as possible. Grandma preferred quiet, and Winnie was anything but. She was boisterous and outgoing, with a heart of gold that Jules treasured.

They'd met in sixth grade during cheerleading try-outs. Jules, the shy gangly girl who towered over everyone else; Winnie, the bouncing redhead who couldn't stand still. They were assigned to the same try-out group, which meant they would go in together to show the judges their memorized routine. Jules had been nervously practicing by the trophy case, stealing glances at her reflection in the glass, when Winnie appeared, breathless and eager.

"Hey, we're in the same group! Let's practice. I want to look in sync. I'm Winnie, by the way. You're Jules, right?" she blurted, hand outstretched.

They both made the squad, and that was that: Jules and Winnie became inseparable all through high school. You didn't get one without the other, up until Jules moved away for college and eventually D.C., while Winnie stayed in their hometown, earning her teaching degree online. Now, she taught English at the same high school. Jules thought this was a little ironic because Winnie skipped more school than she attended. Even so, she was incredibly smart, and Jules knew her students loved her. How could they not?

Before grabbing her bags, Jules took a deep breath, feeling a sense of relief to be here. Seeing the only house she ever called home felt like a big hug she didn't realize she needed. It was classical-looking, with four large white pillars flanking the front door that held up a decorative balcony on the second floor.

Now, all the front windows were open and the red brick almost glowed in the late summer sunset. It had been in Grandpa Lou's family since the mid-nineteenth century. His great aunt and uncle built it when Riverbend was nothing but farmland. Not much had changed since then, except an addition of a downtown area that now serviced its fifteen thousand residents and the highway connecting it to Chicago.

Barb helped Jules wrangle her luggage up the front steps, stopping abruptly at the front door.

"This is as far as I go, Hun," she said.

Jules set her bag down, turning to face her. "I thought you guys would have made up by now. It's been a year since you moved out."

"Afraid not, my dear. She still won't take my calls. Occasionally, I get a thumbs-up emoji text just so I know she's still alive."

A year ago, Barb moved out again to be closer to her boyfriend, causing a huge rift between her and Grandma Rosa. Jules understood her grandma's frustration. This wasn't Barb's first time pulling a stunt like that and leaving for a whirlwind romance. She knew it was only time before she'd come back after the inevitable breakup. By now, Grandma Rosa couldn't understand why Barb didn't just swear off men and embrace a "Grey Gardens" life with her instead. Jules suspected her grandma's loneliness might be at play. Barb had never stayed away this long before.

Jules thanked Barb for the ride, giving her a tight smile and a hug before stepping inside the small foyer lined with oil paintings of Italian countryside landscapes. Bending over to slip her shoes off, a whiff of something baking in the oven danced in the air, beckoning her inside. The smell hit her like a memory: warm, sweet, and familiar. She smiled to herself. Molasses cookies. Her favorite.

She rounded the corner through the formal dining room that boasted an original buffet built for the house and a large table that was always set with her grandma's finest chinaware. Jules ran her hand along the green silk tablecloth as she turned the corner into a small but efficient kitchen.

It hadn't changed much. Still painted yellow, with a compact white farm-style kitchen sink as the focal point. The refrigerator was the same, a time capsule from the sixties, but still humming along. Just seeing the kitchen made her shoulders relax a little, and she felt exhaustion creep up her spine, like it had been waiting for permission.

"Jules!" Winnie squealed, louder than necessary as she dropped the cookies she'd just pulled from the oven on the counter, rushing to wrap her in a dramatic hug. Winnie rarely respected Jules' preference for personal space, but, truth be told, Jules didn't mind.

Jules spotted her petite, yet always flawlessly dressed grandma sipping her coffee, perched on a chair at the square table pushed against the far wall. Her chestnut brown and grey hair was up in the tight French twist she always wore, but exhaustion etched across her face, even though she tried to hide it behind makeup. Jules could see Rosa's expression over Winnie's shoulder, eyes wide, pleading for a rescue. Jules gave her grandma a timid hug, careful not to bump her bad hip.

"You don't have to handle me like a precious teacup, you know," her grandma teased after they settled around the table. "If you do, it'll be a long month for the both of us."

"I know. I'm just being cautious. Everyone knows you can take care of yourself. I'm just here for the company," Jules explained.

The conversation quickly turned to Jules and her trip, which she recounted, leaving out the work details. Her grandma didn't understand what Jules did for a living. She couldn't believe that famous people, especially politicians, didn't write their own speeches. Jules had given up long ago trying to explain it to her.

"Well, I, for one, am so glad you're home," chimed Winnie. "Speaking of, I could use some help tomorrow if you have the time."

Preparing herself for any number of wild things Winnie might try to rope Jules into, she asked for more details, knowing full well that she'd do it, regardless.

When they were teenagers, Winnie convinced her they should get jobs at the local roller rink even though neither of them could skate. Jules ended up with two broken fingers after a few kids at a birthday party ran her over on the rink, but she got free pizza and soda out of the deal, so she still counted it as a win.

"I'm acting as the director for the next school play. We're doing *Our Town* and need help setting up the stage design. I asked for volunteers, but didn't get many takers. Only three scrawny, typical theater kids. So, I need all the hands I can get," she explained.

Chapter 2

The next morning, Jules drove to Riverbend High School in her grandparents' old Subaru Outback. She still knew the school like the back of her hand. It hadn't changed much in the time she'd been gone.

Parking next to Winnie's beetle, she headed through the performing arts center entrance to the theater like she'd done thousands of times in another life. Inside the dimly lit space, she paused at the back, eyes adjusting to the shadows. Onstage, a few scrawny kids, smaller than they should've been for their age, were struggling to shove a street-shop set piece into position. This was going to be a long morning.

Out of the corner of her eye, she saw Winnie bounce through a side door, two big boxes balanced in her arms, and Jules rushed to help.

"Thank God you're here," Winnie said. "Can you go to the band room and help bring the boxes in there to backstage? We have a lot to assemble."

Jules saluted, heading towards the band room where she'd spent many hours practicing her flute in high school. Walking down the hall from the theater towards the classroom, a wave of nostalgia hit her. She didn't know how Winnie could stand to be in this school every day, with all its memories floating around, ready to strike.

Staring down the empty hall, she could almost hear the echoes of her former high school bandmates shouting, "GOOO Bears!" as they lined up in the hallway in their green and blue marching uniforms, ready to rush the football field to play the school's fight song before the Friday night game.

Jules smiled at the memory. Band had been her happy place in high school. Her cheerleading days didn't last past middle school, but she didn't mind. She found her tribe in eighth grade with the band kids and even more so after Miles walked into her life on the first day of freshman year.

Too bad she couldn't think about high school, even now, without that familiar pang of hurt.

Miles had changed everything for her. The moment he strode into band class, his long brown curly hair flopping over his forehead and saxophone case thrown over his shoulder, she knew she was in trouble. He looked like he'd just walked off the cover of *Rolling Stone*.

Their band teacher, Mr. Fedema, had introduced him, informing the class he had moved to Riverbend from Chicago that summer. Jules stared at Miles as he took his seat one row over. She'd never seen someone look so effortlessly cool.

He must have felt eyes on him, because he jerked his head over to where she sat, returning her stare. Startled, Jules had looked away, embarrassed at being caught. She wanted to melt into the floor right then and there.

After class, Miles approached her as she packed up her flute. "What's your name?"

Jules momentarily lost her ability to speak and croaked out, "Jules," before bolting to the door, heart racing. The scene played over in her head hundreds of times during the rest of that day, fresh embarrassment blooming each time. She felt like a bumbling idiot and not the confident, worldly high schooler she'd imagined all summer.

But Miles wouldn't give up. Every day after band, he walked her to her next class in silence. Soon, rumors started they were hooking up, even though that was far from the truth. They hadn't said more than five words to each other.

It got so bad that one day Winnie walked up to Miles and demanded that he either ask Jules out or stop messing around. She told him she wouldn't "let her best friend get stalked by a psycho killer." Miles asked her to the movies that afternoon.

After that, they fell into an easy but sometimes all-consuming relationship. He was her rock and she his. Neither of them had great home lives, which bonded them, in a way. They were even crowned homecoming king and queen one year, not that either of them cared about things like that, although they agreed it might make a funny story one day.

Everything felt like it fit, right until the night of their senior prom, where it had gone painfully wrong. Four years of memories and first love forever tarnished in Jules' mind.

Not that she ever talked about it with anyone. No one knew exactly what happened that night; just that they broke up and Jules moved away early for college and Miles spent a few days behind bars in county lockup. Jules never even learned the full story, because she didn't care to know the details. She knew enough—he'd ghosted her on prom night and ended up ruining his future.

Opening the door to the band room, she chastised herself for thinking about Miles. She was thirty now and what happened between them was more than a decade ago. She'd almost gotten married since then. She shouldn't be hung up on this. The next few hours flew by as she helped Winnie and their rag-tag team of teen thespians unpack boxes and get the stage ready for rehearsals.

When they finished, Jules worked on breaking down the cardboard boxes for recycling. Exhaustion and hunger gnawed at her, so she heaved the pile of boxes into her arms, hoping to only make one trip to the dumpster outside. It was a risky bet, but the thought of the leftover goulash she cooked for dinner last night made it worth the gamble. The sooner she finished, the sooner she could go home and dig in.

Balancing the flattened boxes in her arms, Jules turned down the short set of steps leading outside, careful to keep her footing as she descended to the garbage area. Unfortunately, she miscounted how many steps were left and missed the last one, dropping the boxes as she stumbled, twisting her ankle on the concrete.

"Shit, shit, shit," she cursed, looking down at the boxes. Jules tried to put weight on her throbbing ankle, wincing as she stood. *What a mess*, she thought.

Just then, she heard the door open behind her.

"Jules?" came a deep voice from the top of the short staircase.

She spun around as quickly as she could on her hurt ankle. A tall man holding a garbage bag stared down at her. For a moment, her brain short-circuited until she realized who it was.

Miles.

Well, an older, and frustratingly more handsome, version of Miles than she remembered.

"Miles," she said, breathier than intended. They stared for a moment, each examining each other. It had been over twelve years since they were face-to-face.

His dark brown curly hair was now shorter on the sides and long on the top, with wisps of grey peeking through. A slight five o'clock shadow highlighted his strong jaw line and his piercing green eyes still complimented his olive-colored skin. He was no longer the long lanky teen she remembered; his frame had filled out and she could see his wide shoulder and chest muscles through his black t-shirt. *He definitely spent time in the gym*, she thought.

Blinking her eyes to focus and covering her forehead with her hand to block the mid-day sun, she thought her mind was playing tricks on her. Had her memories conjured him up? He couldn't really be here. Last she'd heard, he was living in Detroit or Minnesota or somewhere like that.

"Looks like you could use some help," he said, breaking the trance.

"With what?" Jules asked after a beat. It came out a bit rude, but she was too shocked to function properly.

He swept a hand, gesturing towards the mess of cardboard behind her. "Oh, that. I can handle it. Just lost my balance."

"I guess some things never change."

Yeah, it was Miles.

"What does that mean?" Jules shot back, suddenly self-conscious and a little embarrassed to be found in this situation.

"You were always a little clumsy, that's all," he said, jogging down the stairs to help her pick up the boxes.

"You don't have to do that. It's the last of them, anyways. I was just helping Winnie out in the theater," Jules tried to explain.

"Let me help. Looks like you hurt your ankle."

That was one thing Jules remembered about Miles; he was always ready to help anyone in need, even if it meant that he'd be late to class, miss band practice, or not show up on time to pick her up. Once, he was late picking her up for a football game because he'd been helping his elderly neighbor search for her missing cat, only to find out from the woman's daughter that the cat had died a month earlier. Miles still promised his neighbor that they'd look more the next day. Which they did, for three hours.

Jules used to love that about him, but now she knew better. After everything that happened between them all those years ago, she didn't know who he was anymore.

Before she could respond, he began picking up the boxes and throwing them in the bin.

"Thanks," she said, watching him.

"No problem. Need some help getting back inside?"

"Sure."

He wrapped his arm around her back to steady her.

She didn't want to be close to him, but she didn't have a choice. Her ankle still throbbed. As they hobbled up the steps, Jules took in his scent, a mix of sweet sandalwood and a musky spice she could never quite place. He smelled like he always had, and it was intoxicating. She caught herself taking another deep inhale and abruptly stopped walking, snapping back to reality.

"I got it from here. Thanks," she said, hurrying away from him and hobbling down the rest of the hallway, using the wall for support. Admittedly, it wasn't the sexiest she'd ever looked, waddling away from him like a gimp. But she had to put distance between them, the mix of emotions swirling in her chest made her vision blurry. *Why was he here?*

"Great seeing you, too, Jules," he called behind her.

After they cleaned up backstage, Winnie followed Jules back to her grandma's house for lunch. It had been two years since she'd seen her best friend in person, although they FaceTimed every Sunday night. It was the most consistent date night Jules had since her breakup with Luke. And now, Jules had some questions for Winnie, Miles-related.

Once home, Jules warmed up the goulash and helped her grandma downstairs to the kitchen to eat with them before putting an ice pack on her ankle, which already felt better. She was going to have to tell them both about running into Miles, although part of her still thought she might have imagined it all.

Jules knew it would make her grandma's day. Rosa always loved Miles. She still tried to bring him up occasionally, even though Jules always shut the conversation down as quickly as it started. Winnie, however, never mentioned him by name anymore. She knew better.

After what happened their senior year, Winnie would go on and on about what an asshole he was for standing her up on prom night, even though that's not exactly what happened. Jules would never admit it but she appreciated that Winnie had her back. At least someone understood.

Once they were at the table eating, Jules wanted answers.

"So, I didn't realize Miles was still in town."

Winnie stopped with her fork halfway to her mouth, thinking for a moment before answering, "Yeah, he's been back for a little while. I don't see him much." She shrugged her shoulders.

"Interesting. I saw he was wearing a school staff badge." Jules tried not to sound accusatory.

"You saw *Miles*?" her grandma interrupted with too much enthusiasm.

Jules told them a quick version of what happened while they ate. As she spoke, she could sense Winnie was holding back. Winnie wore her emotions on her sleeve, so it was easy to know what she was feeling. Normally, Jules loved that about her, but right now it felt like she was on the outside, missing a piece of important information.

"He's the new band instructor for the high school. He's been back for about a year now," Winnie cooly explained, trying not to make a big deal of it.

"Did you know he was back?" Jules asked her grandma.

"*Maybe...*" she said with a wink. "I might have heard something about it. I tried to tell you a few months ago, but you cut me off before I could finish."

"And you didn't think to warn me before I went to the school today?" she asked them both.

"Honestly, I didn't think you'd even care," Winnie said. "You haven't brought him up in years."

Rosa only shrugged.

"Well, I'm happy for him," Jules said in a contrite tone as she gathered the bowls and brought them to the sink to rinse. "I'm glad he didn't waste his life, after all."

She was confused, and maybe jealous? Whatever she was feeling, she wanted it to stop. It was hard to pretend that seeing him didn't rattle her today. For over a decade, she'd worked hard to push that time in her life as far away as possible. She even moved across the country to prove that she could make it on her own, broken heart and all. And now he was back apparently, and all seemed to be forgiven.

Sitting in that cozy kitchen, Jules felt the dormant anger and hurt stir inside. Sure, the rational part of her knew Miles deserved a good life. They were so young when everything happened. But it didn't change the fact that what he did that night not only ruined his own plans, he'd also destroyed the little trust she had in other people.

"Well, let's change the subject," she said. "What's on the agenda for this week?"

Chapter 3

With the house quiet, Winnie gone, and her grandma napping upstairs, Jules sat alone, replaying the night before, the sharp sting of forgetting a recipe she once knew by heart still lingered.

***

"Jules! Let's whip up some goulash for dinner," her grandma called up the stairs to where Jules was unpacking her bags.

Jules hadn't made a fresh meal from scratch in years, and a pang of anxiety flashed through her mind. Her meals mostly consisted of take-out or pasta from a box and a can of tomato sauce. She doubted she'd be able to "whip up" much else.

Jules made her way back to the kitchen but lingered near the table, hoping her grandma would give her a clue to what she needed to make the dish, afraid to admit she couldn't recall the exact ingredients and steps. Although they'd made it together dozens of times growing up, she wracked her brain to remember. Maybe peppers and some kind of noodle?

Sensing her hesitation, Grandma Rosa told her where to find the ingredients in the pantry and refrigerator.

"I had some groceries delivered before you got here," she explained. "There's fresh pasta from John's Shoppe, too," her grandma instructed.

John's Italian Shoppe was a fixture in Riverbend. It had been around since the town first incorporated decades ago. Located in the center of Main Street downtown, it donned an iconic green and white striped awning out front and a few cute wrought-iron tables where people sat to eat fresh gelato in the summer months. Every Saturday morning growing up, her grandma would take Jules there to pick up fresh bread and pasta flour. Boxed pasta just wouldn't do. Not even on the days when her grandma's arthritis flared, stiffening her hands.

Jules found the ingredients where Rosa said they'd be, and soon the recipe came back to her in bits and pieces. It had felt good to cook again, especially in the kitchen where she learned how, even if she was a little rusty from being out of practice. Maybe she could teach herself again, dust off her skills while she was home.

In the end, the goulash tasted good, but it wasn't her grandma's. Jules swore Grandma Rosa used secret ingredients in her recipes. Nevertheless, they'd both enjoyed the meal. It reminded her of the many hours they used to spend in this kitchen together years ago.

Cooking in this kitchen was home.

***

The previous night's struggle to make a dish as simple as goulash got under Jules' skin. Determined to feel useful, she pulled herself back from the memory to the kitchen table where she still sat as the as the afternoon heat seeped in through the cracked windows. She needed to move, to do anything but sit there.

As she stood to rinse out the lunch dishes, she heard a faint drip coming from the sink. Curious, she fiddled with the handle, turning it on and then off again. The dripping didn't stop. Hoisting herself beneath the sink, Jules found a large bucket catching a steady leak from the seams on the pipes. This would give her something to do, although she had zero idea what the parts were called, or how to fix it, but she wanted to try. *How hard could tightening a leaky sink be?*

"Damn thing," Rosa muttered as the front wheel of her walker caught on the kitchen doorway, startling Jules. She hadn't heard her wake up.

"What are you doing under there?"

"Just looking around," she said, pushing herself upright and not wanting to elaborate further. Jules knew her grandma would try to talk her out of fixing the sink herself.

"Mm-hmm. Whatever you say," her grandma murmured as Jules tried to help her to the table only to be waved off. Rosa wasn't one to admit defeat.

"I'm going to head to the store for some more groceries. Text me if you want anything," Jules said, grabbing her bag and keys to the Subaru before kissing her grandma and heading out the door.

It was a short drive downtown, one she could maneuver blindfolded. But this time, Jules slowed down as she turned onto Main Street. A lot had changed since she'd last been there.

The Piggly Wiggly was now a Jewel-Osco, the old sandwich joint had turned into a coffee shop boasting planter boxes of colorful flowers, and the Post Office had moved to another shopping center altogether. Thankfully, Nicholson's hardware store was in the same location it always had been, right next to John's Italian Shoppe.

Snagging a parking spot in front, Jules made her way into John's Shoppe, eager to see if it had changed at all.

The layout was different, but it still had that fresh baked bread smell that she loved as a kid. The narrow aisles donned shelves full of fresh and imported ingredients, many from Italy. Soon, she found herself standing in front of the dessert case and picked out a dozen Italian cookies, her favorite.

After sneaking a bite of cookie, she wandered through the store, pushing a half-sized cart, trying to decide what she should cook for dinner. Grandma Rosa hadn't texted her, so she was on her own.

Inspired by the variety of ingredients around her, ideas were toppling over themselves as she felt a spark of creativity for the first time in a while. It didn't take long to fill her cart to the brim.

"You've got quite the collection of food here," the store's cashier commented after Jules had made her way to the only till.

Jules shrugged. She probably went overboard, but she didn't want to limit herself. The thought of cooking made her excited to get back in the kitchen. And she wanted to redeem herself for last night's sad performance. Satisfied with her purchases, Jules loaded the bags into the car and made her way to Nicholson's. Her sore ankle throbbed a little, reminding her to go slow.

The clean and organized hardware store smelled like paint and pine wood and was illuminated by bright LED lights hanging overhead. Standing just inside the front glass doors, Jules scanned back and forth, looking for anyone who could help; she had no idea where to start. Losing hope in finding someone who worked there, she took her time navigating to the plumbing section using the aisle signs that hung from the ceiling. Nothing looked familiar to her as she stared blankly at the various tools and parts hanging from the rack. With a grunt, she pulled her phone out of her purse and punched "how to fix a leaking sink" into Google where she found several articles detailing what she'd need and how to do it.

Back at home, Jules put away the groceries and laid out the tools and parts she purchased on the counter to take inventory. All of her motivation disappeared.

"What's all this?" Grandma Rosa asked, taking in the sight.

"The sink is leaking, so I went to Nicholson's to get a few things. I'll tackle it tomorrow," she said, biting the inside of her cheek.

"Baby girl, that's not your job. I can hire someone to do that."

'Baby girl' was the nickname Grandma Rosa used for her whenever she was trying to be sensitive or cheer her up. Hearing it now, Jules felt tender towards her grandma, especially knowing she never had to worry about things like leaking sinks when Grandpa Lou was alive. He took care of her this way, always putzing around the house to fix it up. It was his pride and joy.

The thought made her even more determined. She didn't want her grandma worrying about a silly sink. Plus, if she was going to be here, she needed to be helpful.

"Let me just try. I googled how to do it. God knows there are plenty of other things around the house that could use a professional. Like the ceiling fans upstairs that won't turn on."

"Oh, you *googled it*, I stand corrected. You are now a certified plumber," her grandma teased with a wink. Jules just rolled her eyes and shook her head. She'd figure it out.

Jules gathered the spaghetti, pancetta, and cheese she had picked up from John's earlier to make dinner.

Grandma Rosa guessed right away it was for spaghetti carbonara. They'd made it hundreds of times together, so Jules knew she wouldn't need her grandma's help this time. She could make it in her sleep and hoped her grandma would sit back and relax, but Jules should have known better. At every step, Rosa chimed in, "Are you going to grate the cheese by hand?" or "You're not going to use cream, right, just pasta water like I taught you?"

It slowed Jules down, but she didn't mind. She loved being back in this kitchen cooking with her grandma. It felt more natural to her than anything had in years. And it tasted delicious.

As a child, Jules always thought she'd go to culinary school and work her way to becoming a successful chef, taking the food world by storm. No doubt in her mind that she'd make it happen, just like her great grandfather. But as with most childhood dreams, its shine faded, reality eclipsing its allure.

Jules didn't realize her family wasn't "normal" until she entered middle school. Her family didn't look like the other nuclear families around her. Sure, she had a mom, but she was hardly ever around, and she never knew her father. Her mom didn't say much about him, except that he left when Jules was three months old. As she grew older, Jules learned she could only depend on a few people: her grandparents and herself. That's when her dreams of becoming a celebrated chef faded into the rearview mirror.

Jules knew she had to be strong and sensible, because no one was going to save her. And that meant going to college, getting a degree, and then a respectable and safe job. She wasn't willing to gamble stability on a childish dream.

After dinner, they sat upstairs together in the TV room in their pajamas, watching a *Lifetime* movie. Jules was transported back to being the eleven-year-old little girl who used to spend many nights up here doing the same thing. She loved these simple evenings with her family.

"You know, I've missed cooking with you," her grandma said during a commercial break, almost reading her mind. "But it seems like you don't do much of it on your own."

"Is it that obvious?" Jules asked. "I don't really have time for it and it's just me now, anyway."

"Hmm." Jules felt her grandma hesitate, not wanting to offend her. "Well, I'm glad you're here to cook for us," Rosa added.

"Me, too." She was glad. It felt good.

"You know, I have a box full of old recipes that I haven't made in years. I was going to work my way through them this year. You know, before I became helpless," she said gesturing to her hip.

"You'll never be helpless. I bet you can get through the recipes by Christmastime."

"I have a better idea. Maybe we could do it together, while you're here?" she asked, looking at Jules. "It would give me an activity to focus on. A person can only watch so much *Lifetime* before their mind turns to mush."

Jules took a moment to think before saying anything. She thought maybe her grandma was offering more for Jules' benefit than her own, but it *would* give her something to do besides playing caretaker and worrying about her career, not to mention all her life choices leading up to this. There was nothing like idle time to make a person spiral into doubt and anxiety, which is why she always kept herself busy.

"Sure, let's do it. On one condition, though. I don't want an overly pushy sous chef in the kitchen with me," Jules agreed, winking at her grandma.

"Pff, sous chef, my ass! I haven't been a sous chef since the early 1950s when I started working at my dad's restaurant in Chicago." Grandma Rosa laughed, tossing her hand over her shoulder. They stayed huddled together on the couch until the movie finished and their eyes were heavy with sleep.

The next morning, as they were drinking their coffee, Grandma Rosa told Jules where to find the recipe box. It was hidden in the back of the cupboard pantry, behind cans of tomato sauce and olives that might have been older than her. The shoe-box-sized tin was rusty at the hinges with a 1970s orange and green floral pattern around the outside. Inside, dozens of yellowing index cards containing recipes written in her grandma's handwriting were stacked together. Jules wondered when she started saving these. She'd never seen or heard of this box before last night, but it had clearly been around long before she was born.

Dusting off the box, Jules sat it on the table between them.

"When did you start collecting recipes? They look ancient," she asked, flipping through the cards.

"Around the time that your mom went to grade school. I had a lot more time on my hands then, so I started experimenting in the kitchen. Some recipes were better than others, but your grandpa Lou loved it. He got to try different dishes almost every night for five years straight," she told Jules with a half chuckle.

Jules didn't realize that the recipes in the tin were originals and not recipes she copied down from other places. She was impressed. She knew her grandma loved to cook, but never considered Rosa might have been a woman with a serious passion, not just a housewife who knew her way around the kitchen.

"Why did you stop?" she asked.

"It wasn't just one thing, I guess. Life got harder. Your mom grew into an angsty teenager who needed more attention. For a long time, it reminded me of a dream that never came true, so I stopped. Sometimes what you love can also make you deeply unhappy with yourself."

Jules knew that feeling. Lately, writing made her unhappy. In college, she felt drawn to it because it allowed her to create within a structured system. The rules of language made her feel grounded and in control. Not like she was floating in an abyss of possibilities that she'd never find her way through, like many other creative endeavors she never mastered. But now, she often felt too boxed in by it. Maybe she wasn't good enough or didn't have enough passion for writing to fill an entire career.

"So why now? Why do you want to revisit them?" Jules asked, referencing the recipes in the box.

"A lot of time has passed since then and I can't quite remember the woman I was when I made them. I'd like to revisit her again."

Chapter 4

Before Jules could cook another thing in this kitchen, the sink would have to be fixed. It would drive her crazy knowing it was still leaking if she spent any more time in here than she already had.

Determined to do it herself, she climbed underneath, armed with YouTube, and tinkered around with the tools she bought yesterday.

It only took a few minutes to realize she might be in over her head. After tightening and loosening various nobs and screw-y looking parts on the pipe, she took a quick break to wipe off the beads of sweat forming on her forehead and to see if she'd made it any better. Turning the faucet back on, Jules held her breath. To her horror, water spurted out of the pipe in all directions. She'd made it worse. A lot worse.

"Fuck," she shouted. Jules always had a bit of a potty mouth on her. She rushed to turn it off and clean up the mess before grabbing the car keys to head back to the hardware store. Maybe this time, they could recommend a good plumber.

As she turned into the parking lot in front of Nicholson's, Jules was forced to maneuver her car around a large white pickup truck, annoyed that someone thought they were special enough to take up two prime parking spaces with their obnoxious vehicle. You'd never see a pickup truck in D.C. unless it was a delivery vehicle. Most people didn't even own cars, let alone a monstrosity that large.

Shaking her head, she walked past the truck and stepped inside, making the doorbell jingle, which must have been broken yesterday. This time, two employees greeted her wearing colored vests, eager to be saved from the afternoon boredom.

The older of the two men led her back to the plumbing section, determined to help her fix the sink without calling a plumber. Apparently, he had a thing against plumbers and handymen, going on and on about how anyone with more than two brain cells could figure out how to take care of their home. Unfortunately for him, Jules wasn't one of them; she'd never owned a home. Of all the places she'd lived since high school, they were all rentals, so she always had a landlord for these sorts of issues. Jules regretted her decision to come back instead of admitting defeat and finding a professional online.

Just as they rounded the corner of the paint aisle into plumbing, she felt the hairs on the back of her neck stick up. A deep, low voice reverberated through the store, one she'd heard just yesterday and had featured heavily in her dreams last night.

Miles was here, of all places. She knew Riverbend was small, but *this* small? Come on.

Jules slowed her pace behind the Nicholson's employee to buy some time. Should she leave? Turn around and hop back in her car? Her mind said to run, but her body moved towards his voice.

Sure enough, there he stood, phone up to his ear in the middle of the plumbing aisle.

"Yeah, I'll come by later tonight," she heard him say into the phone before hanging up.

"Miles, back so soon? Weren't you here this morning?" the Nicholson's employee asked as they walked up.

Jules stood behind the guy, hoping Miles wouldn't see her, but not trying to look suspicious either. *Be casual*, she thought to herself. *Don't make this weird.*

"Hey, Mike. Renovating this house will be the death of me and my wallet," he responded, grabbing a package of unrecognizable white plastic parts that hung in front of him. "I need some more O-rings for the bathroom sink installation."

When he turned around to leave, she caught sight of his face under his battered blue ball cap. He looked tired, yet still as handsome as yesterday. He took a step forward to leave and spotted her, cracking a crooked smile that shot a sharp pang straight to Jules' heart. The corners of his eyes creased in a way that they hadn't years ago, and it made him even more attractive.

Why was her body reacting like this? She needed to get herself under control; she wasn't a lovesick teenager anymore. She was a goddamn grown woman.

"Jules, what are you doing here?" he asked, trapping her in the aisle.

"She's having some trouble with a leaky kitchen sink. Figured I'd try to help her before spending a fortune on a plumber. They'd try to take a young pretty woman like her to the bank, ya' know?" Mike responded before Jules could get a word out.

Jules cringed.

"Is this at your grandma's house?" Miles asked, ignoring Mike.

Jules nodded. "Her sink has been leaking, so I thought I'd try to fix it while I'm here. Turns out I'm no plumber," she said with a sarcastic smile.

"Hmm, I could come take a look. I'm not a professional either, but I might be able to handle a leaking sink."

Mike cut in again, explaining that Miles had been renovating an old house in town by himself. "He knows what he's doing, even if he is all self-taught," he finished with a wink. He sure had a way with words.

Jules hesitated for a moment. Sure, it wouldn't hurt to have a second opinion, especially after she'd made an even bigger mess of things earlier. But the feminist in her screamed she didn't need a man swooping in to save the day. She could handle a leaky sink herself, right?

"Thanks, but I think I've got it," she replied. "This seems to be the easiest of the issues that need fixing around that house."

"It wouldn't be a problem. I could use a break from my own projects," Miles said, waving the package of O-rings in his hand. He wasn't giving up, and Jules didn't want to come off rude again like she had yesterday.

"Plus, you have a bum ankle."

"Oh, yeah. Well, my ankle is fine now," Jules said in a flustered voice. She'd almost forgotten about it. The swelling had all but disappeared. "Just needed some ice and a night of rest. But I guess it wouldn't hurt to have another set of eyes on the sink," she gave in. "When can you swing by?"

"Glad to hear it. How about now?"

Jules couldn't think of a reason why not.

On the drive home, with Miles following in his obnoxious white pickup truck, she checked herself slyly in the mirror. She wasn't expecting to see anyone she knew at the hardware store, let alone Miles. Again. Thankfully, she had brushed her hair and put on some mascara this morning out of habit. She never felt fully awake until she had tamed her hair and washed her face. It was a habit she'd picked up from the other Cuccia women in her family over the years.

Nervous energy pulsed through her as they arrived at the house. *Maybe this wasn't such a good idea*, she thought. She desperately hoped her grandma was napping because she did not want to answer a thousand questions about this later.

Once in the house with Miles lying halfway under the sink, Jules didn't know what to do with herself. Should she sit? Stand? Nothing seemed appropriate. Just as she leaned casually against the counter, the hem of Miles' shirt rose, exposing the part of his tanned abdomen where his muscles formed a V shape pointing south. Jules' mouth went dry, and her lower belly fluttered.

This was a bad idea.

Still unsure what to do, she slid over to the other side of the kitchen, where he'd be out of direct eyesight, and asked him about the house he was renovating.

"It's the yellow house on Van Buren Street. Well, it used to be yellow, now it's white. The one that had all those tacky garden gnomes out front," he said from under the sink. "I bought it about a year ago and decided to renovate it myself. It's the project that just keeps on giving."

Jules remembered the house. She always wondered where someone could buy so many different gnomes, but mostly why someone would want that many.

"Do you still have the gnomes?"

"I kept a couple. Felt wrong to re-home all the gnomes," he said with a slight chuckle. Clearly, he didn't lose his taste for cheesy jokes.

She couldn't help but wonder if he lived there alone, or maybe with a girlfriend. "Is it just you and the gnomes, then?"

"Nope," he said, still under the sink.

Jules held her breath. Of course, he had a girlfriend, or maybe a *wife*? Why wouldn't he?

But then he added, "There's also my cat, Sir-Toots-A-Lot."

She let out a loud laugh and the breath she was holding.

"Sir-Toots-A-Lot? Like my flute?" she asked, amused.

Back in high school, Miles and Jules came up with silly names for their band instruments. He picked out "Sir-Toots-A-Lot" for her flute and she named his saxophone "Sir-Honks-A-Lot."

"Yeah, well, he farts. A lot. So, the name fits," he replied as he slid back out, not meeting her eyes.

Turns out all the sink needed was a good tightening up. When they tried the tap, the water ran smoothly without leaking. Jules felt a little silly for having him come all the way here just to turn a wrench a few times, but at least it was fixed.

She thanked him, expecting him to start towards the door, instead he turned to face her. Their eyes locked for a long, searing moment. The energy buzzed between them. Jules could feel her heartbeat picking up as her breath grew shallow. They hadn't been alone like this in a long time, and her body was betraying her. Miles took a tentative step in her direction, keeping his gaze fixed on her.

Unsure of the moment, Jules broke eye contact and asked if he wanted anything to drink, turning her back to him to open the refrigerator.

"No, Jules. I don't need anything to drink," Miles purred in his low, deep voice that sent a shiver up her back.

Another few seconds of silence passed between them before he quietly added, "I think I should go." Jules felt a quick stab of disappointment.

"Yeah, I'm sure you have a lot to do with the house and all. Thanks again for your help."

"Anytime," he said as he turned and walked out.

Alone in the kitchen, her thoughts toppled over themselves: *Why did he move back here? Where was he before, and what was he doing? Why was he being so nice to her, and why did she react to him that way?*

Seeing Miles again was a complication. One she had not prepared for. Both times they ran into each other, Jules turned into a bumbling idiot, which was unlike herself. Often, her thoughts were a jumbled mess, but she could always pull off an air of confidence in front of people.

Although she had to admit she enjoyed seeing him, she wouldn't let herself forget what had happened between them years ago. She still felt the sharp hurt rise when she thought of it and was too ashamed to face her own part in the mess. He'd never look at her the same if he knew what she did. Jules was still working on forgiving herself, and she couldn't expect him to do the same. Not to mention what *he* did that night. It was all too messy and best left in the past.

Before she could spiral too deep, a chorus of coughs and sneezes came from upstairs. She met Grandma Rosa at the staircase, helping her down as she continued to sneeze. Her grandma's skin looked ashy grey, and her voice sounded nasally. She had caught a cold. It was probably all the meds she took that lowered her immune system.

"Let me make you some chicken noodle soup," Jules offered.

Her grandma screwed her face up in a disgusted look.

"No, no. If you're going to cook, let's make good use of it." She shook her head. "There's a recipe for my minestrone in the tin. We should have everything we need for it."

Jules did as instructed and got to work chopping the vegetables and boiling the broth. As she cooked, Grandma Rosa told her about how she would cook this soup for Grandpa Lou and Barb whenever they were sick. Jules had it growing up, too.

She remembered a time from grade school when her grandpa picked her up one afternoon after she got sick on the playground. The nurse had called home, trying to get her mom, but she wasn't around. Jules must have been seven or eight at the time, and she felt awful. The kind of stomach bug that made it hard to even move your head without feeling bile rise in your throat.

When they got home, Grandpa Lou had settled her on the couch in the TV room with two big pillows and an orange puke bucket on the floor. He would come in every ten minutes to check on her, worry creasing his face. He was so beside himself, he eventually sat on the floor next to her, watching cartoons with her for hours until she fell asleep.

It made Jules sad to think about, but she was grateful to have had so much time with her grandpa. He always made her feel special and taken care of. Growing up, Grandpa Lou was so present in her life that it never even occurred to her to miss having a dad of her own. Grandpa was there, but now he wasn't. Now, all she had were these memories.

Rosa watched her like a hawk as Jules turned all the chopped vegetables into the pot of broth, stirring often, ensuring they softened but did not get soggy. That was the difference between a fresh homemade soup and a canned, thoughtless soup: the crispness of the veggies. Of course, balanced seasonings helped, too, she reminded Jules, as she arranged the garlic, oregano, parsley, thyme, and more on the counter near the stovetop for her. Grandma Rosa measured nothing, just went off her gut and a lot of tasting as it came together. Jules had a hard time with that; she was a rule follower, so it felt wrong to just eyeball important ingredients. She wanted to follow a system and know that in the end, everything would taste the way it should.

"That's not cooking from the heart," her grandma once had told her years ago when they were making chicken piccata. "Every dish is different, even if they have the same name. Feel what it needs and adjust as you go. Cooking is a lot like life, in that way."

Grandma Rosa could always connect cooking and food to just about anything that was going on in life. Jules had missed that.

They spooned heaping mouthfuls of soup from their bowls, careful not to spill on the fancy tablecloth. It was a symphony of hearty, vibrant flavors and comforting textures, each bite packed with tender carrots, zucchini, celery, and green beans, cooked just enough. The broth, rich and flavorful, balanced the tangy sweetness of ripe tomatoes with the savory depth of vegetable stock and herbs. The final sprinkle of fresh grated parmesan and drizzle of good olive oil took it to the next level, while the subtle heat of red chili flakes gave it a gentle kick. A quick squeeze of lemon at the end brightened the taste and tied it all together.

It was the kind of soup that warmed you from the inside, hearty enough to battle a head cold but light enough to be gentle on your stomach. Even though she had some help, Jules felt a satisfying sense of accomplishment for making such a simple yet delicious meal. It unlocked a dormant part of her soul. She could feel the creative energy flow back through her body, leaving her aching to do more, make more.

Bellies full, they each drifted off to their rooms for the night. Jules settled on her bed, grabbing her computer to check her missed emails. Part of her wanted to see a full inbox, to feel needed outside of Riverbend. Becoming replaceable wasn't an option in her mind.

Her laptop whirred to life after two days of rest. It took a few frustrating minutes to connect to the house Wi-Fi network, which Jules had set up years ago before she moved to D.C. She still remembered the password: BoBo1957, the name of their old dog, plus the year her grandparents got married. At least some things never changed, she thought. Slowly, she watched her inbox tick up with new messages. At the top was an email from Becca's personal account:

Jules-

Hope everything is going well and that you're getting some deserved downtime.

We talked briefly about this before you left, but wanted to remind you to sign your employment contract for the PR firm.

Look it over and shoot me any questions. I've attached it here, again.

I'm so excited to take this next step with you by my side. We'll be unstoppable.

-Becca

Rubbing her eyes to relieve the pressure building behind them, Jules knew she had to review the contract. Just not tonight. It deserved a fresh mind, she rationalized, as a vague attempt to keep putting it off.

It had been over a month since Becca had offered Jules the Chief Communications Officer role, the chance to move into a leadership position. But Jules couldn't bring herself to make it official and sign the papers. Becca was taking an enormous leap by starting her own agency, and Jules admired her for it. But honestly? She was terrified. What if it flopped? What if she sucked at the job? And did she even see herself doing this in a few months, let alone a few years? The whole thing felt way too big to decide tonight. She was exhausted, and her brain was done. A podcast and some sleep sounded much better. The rest of the emails could wait.

As she was dozed off, her phone lit up with a text from Winnie. Jules groaned, but she was used to receiving texts from Winnie at all hours of the day.

> *Hi :) Emily and I are going to the football game on Friday. You're coming with us. It might be fun or just make us feel old! xx*

Winne met Emily on a cruise to the Bahamas five years ago and they'd been inseparable since. Not long after returning from the trip, Emily visited Winnie in Riverbend and never left. It worked for them since Emily was a copy editor and could work from anywhere with an internet connection. While Jules never understood whirlwind romances, she adored Emily. The two of them together were a sight to be seen, a voluptuous redhead and a tall, gorgeous bleach blonde model type. They demanded attention wherever they went. But it was more than that; they balanced each other perfectly. Emily was a calm oasis to Winnie's electric storm of a personality.

Jules sent back a thumbs-up emoji before dozing off into a deep sleep she didn't realize she needed.

Chapter 5

The next few days flew by with Jules falling into a peaceful rhythm, cooking, cleaning, and helping Grandma Rosa, although the list of things needing repairs around the house grew longer each day. Jules needed to call a contractor. The sink had made it painfully clear she was in over her head.

On Friday morning, Winnie rang Jules, "Be ready by four tonight! I'll pick you up after school to pregame the game!"

Jules couldn't decide if she was excited or nervous but decided to go with it. She needed a drink, anyway.

Once back at Winnie's house, the three of them sat on the wood deck that faced a well-manicured garden of white roses and yellow daffodils. Emily and Winnie had bought the charming two-bedroom cottage a few years ago and fixed it up to look like it belonged in a children's fairytale book. They'd painted the outside a soft robins-egg blue and added a charming wooden fence that ran around the front yard, which was lined with plush green bushes and a mix of colorful wildflowers. The front door was painted a bright yellow and tucked back into a tight alcove trimmed with an arch of earth-colored stones.

Out back, they sipped martinis in chilled glasses that seemed too posh and sophisticated for a football tailgate. The weather was perfect, not too hot for an early September day. A slight breeze wafted in pleasant garden aromas while the sun shone bright above without a cloud to be seen.

As they relaxed, Winnie recalled how, just yesterday, two students were caught with their pants down in the janitorial elevator in the school, a rite of passage at Riverbend High. Jules and Miles had even managed it without getting caught their senior year, although she kept that to herself and just smiled as she took a refreshing sip of her martini.

Jules had to admit, spending a Friday afternoon like this fed her soul in a small way that hadn't happened in years. She felt relaxed, her shoulders releasing as the sun warmed her face. Or maybe that was just the alcohol working its magic. Either way, Jules didn't care. She was grateful to be here.

Serving another round of drinks, Emily approached the subject of Miles.

"I heard you ran into your high school sweetheart earlier this week. How was that?" she asked.

Trying to control her voice at the mention of him, Jules answered, "It was fine." Then added, "I just wish someone had warned me he might be lurking around." Jules looked at Winnie with a sarcastic smile. The drinks loosened her up, and she went on to tell them about his visit to the house the other day.

"Actually, I ran into him again, at the hardware store," she admitted. Winnie let out a loud shriek, clapping her hands in front of her.

"And you weren't going to tell me? Why am I just hearing about this now?" she demanded.

"Because it wasn't a big deal. I needed help with the kitchen sink, and he was there. You know his penchant for being a do-gooder," Jules explained.

"You mean he came to the house? Why are you burying the lede?" Winnie's eyes widened with every word.

Fanning disinterest, Jules told them a quick version of the story, leaving out the parts where she couldn't stop looking at his body and the thick tension that made it hard to breathe. Jules still wasn't sure if she'd imagined the last part.

"I should warn you that you'll probably see him again tonight," Emily quipped. "He'll be on the field with the student band, though. So, you'll be a safe distance from him."

For a moment, Jules felt blindsided before realizing the obvious. Of course he'd be there. He was the new band director, after all. Now nervous, the relaxation she felt earlier vanished, replaced by anxious bubbles in her chest that made her body tingle. Was she excited to see him again? No, she had to get a hold of herself. And like Emily said, he'd be busy so he wouldn't even notice her there, anyway.

They finished their drinks and walked to the school, which was just down the street. Even from two blocks away, they could hear music playing from the loudspeaker at the stadium and the low rumble of hundreds of people gathering. Friday night football in Riverbend was a favorite local pastime. Everyone came out to watch the game, young and old. Decades ago, a local wealthy family had donated enough money to build a stadium large enough to hold the whole town and then some.

Entering through the massive brick admissions gate, the green manicured field came into view. It looked the same except for the new stadium lights towering overhead, tall and gleaming. Pep rally activities were in full swing as the cheerleaders led chants on the sidelines with the students lining the front rows of the home team bleachers. The announcer was listing the game stats of the previous years, reminding everyone that the Riverbend Bears almost went undefeated last year until the state championship game, which they vow to avenge this season.

The stands were a sea of the school's colors, blue and green. Some students weren't even wearing shirts and instead had letters painted on their stomachs or chests to spell out "Go Riverbend." It was a sight to be seen, and one that Jules knew well. Not much had changed in the twelve years since she was a student. She could even smell the familiar aroma of their famous porkchop sandwiches wafting in from the concession stand.

"Come on, let's go grab seats before all the good ones are gone," Winnie said, grabbing Jules and Emily's wrists as she weaved through the throngs of people.

It took longer than necessary to get to the bleachers since eager students and parents stopped Winnie every few feet to chat. She was clearly a favorite at the school, given her popularity among the crowd.

Emily gave Jules a shy smile, adding, "It's always like this," before taking Winnie's hand, gazing at her in admiration. Jule's chest tightened with love for them, happy her best friend had found such a good partner.

Once seated, they had a full view of the field. It looked both smaller and larger than she remembered, and the electric buzz of excitement pulsed through her veins. It was hard not to get caught up in the moment. Feeling a burst of school pride, she started chanting along with the rest of the crowd and cheerleaders. She didn't care if it was the two martinis she had earlier. She was going to enjoy the night, win or lose.

Just as Jules got comfortable in her metal seat, a set of doors on the opposite side of the field opened and the band burst through in a ribbon of blue, blasting the school's fight song. Everyone stood and cheered as they marched onto the field in a large V shape, each member outfitted in a navy wool uniform that looked uncomfortable for this warm evening. On her feet and clapping along to the beat, Jules watched, eyes catching on Miles, who stood at the top of the formation, moving his arms to direct the music. His jaw was set tight, focusing on the music and the band. A spike of energy ran through her body, impressed with the sense of ease and confidence he displayed.

In an instant, she was back in high school, marching alongside him on the same field. She remembered how the rush of the moment made her feel alive, how the music vibrated through their bodies, connecting them in a way that made it feel as though they were each a minor part of a larger, living thing. Thinking about it here made the hairs on the back of her neck stand up and her skin broke out in tiny goosebumps. She'd forgotten how much she loved Friday night football games.

At most high schools, being in the band meant you were unpopular or nerdy, but not at Riverbend High. It meant bragging rights. To even get an invitation to try out for the band was a compliment, let alone make the cut. Riverbend's marching band competed state-wide, winning the state championship almost every year and always ranking in the top ten nationally. Between its strong football program and award-winning marching band, it's no wonder the entire town turned out for every home game.

And now Miles led the band. She'd always thought he'd do great things; he received a full-ride scholarship to Oberlin College for its renowned music program. A gifted musician and scary smart to boot, Miles scored almost perfect on his SATs. But then prom night happened senior year, and his scholarship disappeared.

Since then, Jules often wondered if he still played music. He had no social media to speak of and no family left in Riverbend to share any news. But it turned out he didn't give up his love for music, although she doubted Riverbend was his first choice to build a career. Years ago, he'd dreamt of playing in a large city philharmonic. Nevertheless, it suited him. He looked in control and at home on the field.

With the game starting and Jules buzzing from head to toe with nostalgia and school pride, the three of them blended into the frenzied crowd, cheering along at every catch and touchdown. When halftime came, the show the marching band put on blew her socks off. They played "Eye of the Tiger" by Survivor and Katy Perry's "Fireworks" while marching around the field, forming the shape of fireworks and even a cat eye that blinked. It was well worth the eight dollar admission charge.

After the game finished with Riverbend winning by over twenty points, Winnie, Emily, and Jules headed for the exits.

"I forgot how much fun these football games are!" Jules shouted over the noise of the crowd as they shuffled forward towards the exit.

"Best thing to do in Riverbend on a Friday night," Winnie yelled back in between greeting another onslaught of students and parents.

"But not the only thing to do in Riverbend!" Emily added. "Let's head to the Kernel to grab some food."

"You don't mean The Golden Kernel, do you?" Jules asked, wrinkling up her nose. The Golden Kernel was a dive bar that had been around for decades in Riverbend. She'd only been there once, when she'd been home for Christmas break during college. Out of desperation and sheer boredom, Winnie and Jules found themselves dressed up and heading to the only bar in town. They regretted their decision as soon as they stepped into the dimly lit repurposed barn, hit by the stench of hay mixed with puke, shame, and stale beer. The three old men sitting at the bar whipped their heads around as the door closed with a thud behind them, like a scene from a horror movie. Jules grabbed Winnie's hand and dragged her back out the door. They did not belong there.

"Yeah! It has new owners and looks completely different. It's such a nice place now," Winnie explained. "Their food is great."

"They serve *food*?" Jules wondered aloud as Emily grabbed her arm to pull her through the crowd.

Emily opened the Uber app on her phone and ordered a ride for them. Tonight was full of surprises. She could never have imagined a time when Riverbend would have Uber. Growing up, there had only been one taxicab, driven by a guy named Earl who charged a flat rate of ten dollars to go anywhere within city limits.

Once in the spotless and family friendly minivan that picked them up, Jules called her grandma to check in. Rosa had been expecting a longtime friend to stop by with dinner, so Jules was off caretaking duty for the evening. Her grandma sounded happy but tired and told her to have a great night. Jules felt less guilty knowing she wasn't alone for dinner.

During their short ride, she learned more about the bar. Apparently, a young couple from Chicago bought it two years ago, remodeling it into a sort of gastropub that drew in sizeable crowds on the weekends. Most people loved it, but there was still a group of long-time locals who were not thrilled it was now owned by "city folk" instead of someone from Riverbend, a tale as old as time.

Sliding out of the minivan, Jules looked up at a fancy sign on top of the newly painted barn that flashed, "The Golden Kernel" in yellow glowing light with the phrase, "Riverbend's Hometown Gastropub" painted beneath. A promising start.

There was already a short line of customers dressed in Riverbend's blue and green colors standing near the front entrance hostess stand. A short young woman who wore her hair in two tight buns on either sides of her head and a smart all black jumper and bright white sneakers informed them that there was a thirty-minute wait for a table, but they could check out the bar area for open seats.

The gastropub didn't even look like the same place she and Winnie had visited years ago. To start, it smelled like food. Good food. Inside, the wooden beams had been stained a dark walnut color with black iron fittings at the joints. The renovated bar was a long piece of live edge wood with a dozen rustic-looking backless stools lined up along it. Hanging above the bar was a huge elk head and a couple of deer heads, along with a handful of vintage-looking beer signs. A series of intimate leather booths and four-top tables full of lively customers filled the rest of the space. A small stage stood in the corner near the bar, which was empty except for a tall chair and microphone stand. Jules wondered if they had regular shows or mic nights.

Zipping past Jules and Emily, Winnie grabbed the last three open stools at the bar and motioned for them to join her. As they all sat down, Winnie struck up a conversation with the bartender, who looked like the furthest thing from a Riverbend native. His head was shaved on both sides except for the middle, where three large red spikes stood straight up, gelled into submission. In his earlobes hung gauges the size of silver dollars and tattoos ran up and down his arms, leaving little to no skin showing. Although he looked intimidating at first glance, his wide smile suggested otherwise.

"Jax, this is Jules. She lives in D.C. but is back in town helping her grandma for a while," said Winnie as Jax reached across the bar to shake Jules' hand.

"Nice to finally meet you. Winnie mentioned you a few times. Welcome to the Golden Kernel," replied Jax.

"I hope you've only heard good things," Jules teased.

"I might have shared a few of our young dalliances." Winnie winked at Jules. "Jax and his wife, Roxy, own the Golden Kernel. They're responsible for breathing life back into it. Where's your better half?"

"I'm afraid it's just me manning the bar tonight. Roxy's at home relaxing. Her back was acting up today."

Jax explained Roxy was very pregnant with their first child, and it was wreaking havoc on her back.

"What's your preferred poison, ladies?" Jax asked, grabbing a shaker and tossing a bar rag over his shoulder.

The evening was just what Jules needed, a fun night out with friends. She couldn't believe a hip gastropub existed in Riverbend. And Winnie was right; the food was great. They ordered a bunch of plates to share and devoured every bite. Her favorite, the crispy brussels sprouts, had some sort of sauce on the bottom that was both sweet and salty, topped with toasted sunflower seeds. It reminded her of a dish she might get at a fancy restaurant in D.C. *Impressive and unexpected*, Jules thought.

During a lull, Jules complimented Jax on the food.

"It's usually Roxy back there, running the kitchen. They're all her recipes. She went to culinary school back when we were living in Chicago. That's why we bought this place, so she could open her own restaurant. Much cheaper to do here than in the city," Jax shouted above the music, which had gotten louder since they'd arrived.

Jules felt a twinge of jealously rear its head. That had been her dream once upon a time, too. Turns out, Riverbend could have been an option if she just hadn't been so scared of failure. Her chosen path had been the responsible option: college. And now she had a reliable job that kept her busy and paid well, she reassured herself, squashing the thoughts. She was fine. More than fine.

Just as they were ordering another round of beers, a speaker crackled from the stage. Jules didn't give it much thought until she heard the opening chorus of a song and the hairs on her arms stood up. *It couldn't be...*

Sure enough, Miles was on the stage, strumming a guitar, singing into the microphone and staring directly at her. Heat shot up her entire body. She wasn't even sure what song he was playing, just that he was here and looking at her. His eyes smoldered, appearing darker than she'd remembered. *Was he mad? Or was it just the dim lighting?* Jules couldn't tell. His face looked so intense with his chin lowered, lips almost touching the microphone as his deep, soulful voice lingered in the air. He still had talent oozing from every pore.

The heat in her belly swelled with every breath, eyes still locked. In those few moments that seemed to last hours, the bar faded away to just the two of them. Jules wished she could read his mind, but his expression didn't change, only growing more intense as they continued to stare at each other. *What is happening?*

Taking a swig of her beer to distract herself, Jules forced herself to break his gaze and looked over to Emily, who squeezed her hand.

"Everything ok? Want to step outside for some fresh air?" she asked, noticing the moment between them.

"Good idea," Jules mumbled and followed her to the door.

Once outside on the wrap-around porch, Jules threw her head back to take a deep breath of the humid evening air.

"I'm sorry. We should have warned you. Although, I didn't think he'd be here tonight because of the game and all. He rarely plays on Friday nights," Emily said, shaking her head as she assessed Jules' mental state.

"So, he's a regular here?"

Emily told her that Miles knew Jax from the time they'd spent together in Chicago a few years back. Miles helped him and Roxy fix up the old barn and now played for a few hours almost every Saturday night and sometimes during the week. He'd become somewhat of a small-town celebrity, apparently.

After a few moments breathing in the thick air, Jules felt more like herself, in control and level-headed. This would not derail the fun night she'd been having with her friends. Both she, and Miles were adults and could deal with seeing each other, even if it did throw her off-kilter.

She just wished he'd stop giving her those long, heavy glances. They stirred something deep in her stomach, and she wasn't ready to deal with the emotions it brought back. For all she knew, the looks meant he was still angry with her for leaving town without a word after he ripped their plans apart, reminding her she only had herself and her grandparents to count on.

Miles still stood on the stage singing and strumming his guitar when they walked back to their seats. Jules angled her back to the stage so she wouldn't get distracted by his glances and fell into a friendly argument about who had started the infamous water balloon palooza junior year.

Winnie always argued that she'd started it, but Jules knew the truth. Jules was the one who'd suggested it one night out of sheer boredom. It remained the one and only thing Jules had ever done that involved the police. It was stupid, yet so much fun.

School had just let out for the summer, and they had split a six-pack of Mike's Hard Lemonades when Jules half-heartedly suggested that they take the huge sling Winnie's brother had for launching kickballs and use it to launch water balloons onto the roofs of the houses in Winnie's fancy neighborhood. Not surprisingly, Winnie was in.

Recruiting Winnie's brother, they snuck through the dark neighborhood, darting across backyards holding a bag full of water balloons and the sling. One by one, lights popped on in each of the houses as angry yells came from the windows.

Thankfully, no one caught them in the act and no damage had been done, just loud thuds as each of the balloons smashed onto the roofs. They saw a write-up about it the next day in the county paper as a few people had called the police. Although they could have been in big trouble, it was one of Jules' favorite memories from growing up in Riverbend.

"Did I overhear you talking about water balloon palooza?" came a voice from the back of her chair. Jax reached across the bar and handed Miles a tall glass of ice water.

"Oh, you know about this, too?" Emily asked mocking surprise, eyebrows lifted.

"Worst kept secret in all of Riverbend. If Jules' granddad wasn't police commissioner back then, who knows where these two would have ended up," said Miles, sipping his water to hide a smile.

"No one knew it was us!" shouted Winnie, whipping around in her seat to face him.

"Your brother made sure half the town did."

"That little snitch! He's going to pay for that later."

All of them laughed, knowing that Winnie would do no such thing. She loved her brother and had been his fiercest protector growing up. Even now, although he's a twenty-six-year-old man with a wife and kid of his own, she'd go to battle for him.

"It's last call, folks. Let me know if I can get you anything before you head out," Jax announced.

Emily looked to Winnie, asking if she was ready to leave. "You want to share an Uber, Jules?"

"No, that's ok, I'll get my own," Jules answered, knowing Winnie only asked to make sure Jules was alright riding by herself since they lived on opposite ends of town.

Miles jerked his head in Jules' direction and said, "I can take you. It's on my way."

Jules hesitated. It might not be a good idea, given the way he was looking at her earlier and the fact that she couldn't seem to focus or even breathe when they were alone together.

Could she trust herself not to do or say things she'd regret? The rational part of her brain screamed she should take an Uber home. Nothing good could come of spending more time with Miles. But she couldn't ignore the pull she felt towards him. Maybe she'd go just to prove to herself that she could be normal around him, that they could be friendly. Plus, it always made her uncomfortable to ride in an Uber or taxi alone after a few drinks. She'd listened to too many true crime podcasts.

Before overthinking it, she accepted his ride.

Everyone settled their tabs as Miles packed up his guitar and gear on the stage. Only a few other customers lingered, all getting ready to head home. Quicker than expected, Emily and Winnie's Uber arrived, leaving Jules to wait for Miles with Jax at the bar.

"He's mentioned you a few times, you know," said Jax in a low voice, wiping the bar down. "I get the feeling you broke his heart."

Jules sighed, the corners of her mouth turning down. "I could say the same thing."

Before she could elaborate or probe further, Miles walked up to her side at the bar, motioning towards the door. She said goodbye to Jax and followed Miles to his white pickup truck, hopping up into the front passenger seat. It didn't seem like a vehicle he'd drive. She always pictured him in a vintage coupe or car with more personality. It hit her how much she didn't know him anymore. He had changed, and so had she.

In high school, neither of them had their own vehicles, but Miles borrowed his cousin Ricky's beat-up Chevy Malibu for their date nights. They spent a lot of weekend evenings in that car, parked next to a pond they used to skate on in wintertime when it froze over. Set back from the road down a long gravel path in the woods, it became their hidden lover's lane for the rest of their time together.

"You did a great job on the field tonight," Jules said to break the tension as they drove down the dark country road leading into town. "You looked so comfortable."

"Thanks. It surprised me at first, but I love it. Never thought I'd end up teaching a high school band, let alone back here, but

I'm content with it." Miles kept his eyes on the road, but Jules could see a muscle in his jaw clench as he spoke. "How's the sink holding up? Any more issues?"

"Running like new, thanks to you. Unfortunately, I have a long list of other house projects. Seems like nothing has been fixed since Grandpa Lou died."

It occurred to her he might recommend someone since he was fixing up his own house and helped with the Golden Kernel. "You don't happen to know a handyman around town who could help, do you?"

"I do, but why don't I just come take a look? Can't be that complicated. Plus, it'd save your grandma some money," he offered, taking a quick glance in her direction.

Jules couldn't read him. One minute he glowered at her and the next he offered to help her fix things around the house. Was he playing a game? She didn't want to read too much into it, so she took it at face value.

"Umm, sure. If you don't mind, that'd be great." Out of the corners of her eyes she could see a shy smile spread across his face. "Can you come by tomorrow afternoon? I'll make us all dinner as payment," she added without thinking.

"Sure thing. I can be there around four."

Great. Now she'd have to explain things to her grandma, who would be over the moon with the news of Miles visiting and staying for a meal. Jules swallowed a groan.

Miles parked in front of the old brick house and walked Jules to the front door. *At least he still had his manners.*

Thanking him for the ride, Jules stepped towards the front door, accidentally brushing his upper arm with hers. The electric sensation was undeniable, stopping her in her tracks. Miles must have noticed too, because he shot her a look that pierced the inky night. Not letting it linger, Jules recovered and mumbled a thank you before walking into the house. Resting her head on the cool wood of the door, she took a deep, shaky breath to calm herself. She couldn't deny the unresolved feelings that hovered between them. But was she reading it all wrong? She couldn't be sure Miles felt it, too.

Lying in bed that evening, Jules played the night over in her head. Even if she still had a connection with Miles after all these years, she couldn't do anything about it. He lived here, and she lived a thousand miles away. Bottom line: it was impractical; it wouldn't make sense. Jules was no longer outright angry at him; they were so young when it all happened. It was time to move past it.

She told herself that she'd just act normal and avoid any physical contact when he came over tomorrow. They could be friends; he'd be a great friend, right?

Deep down, Jules knew she was in trouble. She couldn't wait for tomorrow.

Chapter 6

Jules' head pounded with a slight hangover the next morning as she sat across from her grandma at the kitchen table sipping her coffee. She tried to give her a condensed version of her night, casually mentioning that Miles would be coming over to take a look at a few things later. Not wanting to play one hundred questions, she tried as best she could to give her grandma enough details to satisfy, but nothing more.

Luckily, Grandma Rosa had something else on her mind, so she didn't linger too long on the whole Miles situation.

"Baby girl," she started, "When Val was over last night, she brought up a great idea and I wanted to run it by you."

Val was one of Grandma Rosa's longest friends and lived in The Landing, a luxury retirement community that catered to seniors at various stages of aging.

"What is it?" Jules replied, happy to switch topics.

Sitting up tall, she continued, "Well, I told her about our little cooking project and that we keep making entirely too much food for the two of us. She mentioned that a few of the old folks at The Landing can't stop complaining about the food they get from the cafeteria they share."

She stopped to shake her head at the word "cafeteria," as if it was the worst thing in the world. "So, Val suggested we take our leftovers there some nights so a handful of them can enjoy a delicious, home-cooked meal. She hopes it might shut up the old biddies. What'd you think? They'll pay for the ingredients and your time."

"Well, first, Val *is* an old person, so I'm not quite sure she should be calling other people old like it's a bad thing. Second, I'm in. I'd love to help."

With that, they got to work deciding on that evening's menu for the three of them, plus about a dozen or so women with discerning palates. Jules still needed to go to the grocery store before Miles showed up around four o'clock, not to mention take a shower and make herself presentable. With the decision for dinner made, she threw on some jeans and an old band t-shirt before making her way into town.

Scanning the aisles at John's Shoppe for the ingredients to make the pesto gnocchi and fresh focaccia they'd decided on earlier, Jules heard her phone ding from her purse. She'd hadn't looked at it since she left the bar. Not even her usual laps around social media, email, and texts. What was wrong with her?

On the home screen, a text appeared:

> *Hi honey. Would you want to grab lunch tomorrow? I'll drive into town to meet you. We could do Mexican? Xo -Mom*

It used to annoy Jules how her mom would always end her texts with a sign off, like she didn't already know who sent the message, but today she found it was slightly endearing. No one could say Barb wasn't predictable. She punched out a quick response, telling her she could meet around one tomorrow for lunch at Los Ponchos, their favorite (and only) Mexican spot in town.

After hauling the grocery bags into the house and organizing her supplies, Jules got to work mixing the focaccia dough right away. It needed enough time to rise before baking later today. Jules had never made bread from scratch, but she wanted to learn, although her teacher didn't go easy on her. Rosa watched her like a hawk the entire time, insisting she use a spoon to measure out the flour into the measuring cup to ensure she didn't "over pack it," and criticizing the way Jules kneaded the dough. In the end, though, they were both satisfied and left the bowl of dough on the counter to do its thing until they were ready for it later.

The afternoon passed quickly as she showered and tried not to focus on the nerves fluttering in her stomach. She reminded herself that Miles was only coming over to help fix a few things around the house and nothing more. Her grandma would be there, too, which would help ease some of the awkward tension.

Jules also made a mental plan to help keep her busy: she would start cooking dinner while he fixed the ceiling fans upstairs. That way, she wouldn't stare at him like a piece of perfectly cooked meat she wanted to devour, like last time.

Hoping to hide the fact that she was nursing a hangover, Jules curled her hair and applied subtle makeup to cover up the dark circles under her eyes. She wanted it to say, "I tried, but not too hard, and definitely not for you."

Once back downstairs and feeling more alive, Jules tidied up a few things before Miles arrived. Soon, the big grandfather clock in the foyer dinged four, and the doorbell rang right on cue.

"Always on time, always a gentleman," Grandma Rosa quipped, rising out of her seat at the same time Jules dramatically rolled her eyes.

"You better be careful or those might get stuck in the back of your head," she teased.

They both made their way through the dining room and into the foyer, where they welcomed Miles at the door with wide smiles. Jules didn't say anything at first, distracted by how his dark V-neck t-shirt hugged his body in all the right places. His hair was combed back, clearly styled, but not fussy. He looked like he just stepped out of a Carhartt catalog with a large toolbox dangling from his hand and a hammer snug in his belt. Their eyes met for a brief second and her body pulsed with a warm, tingling feeling.

Tools and hammer, Jules. He came to work, not be ogled at, she silently chastised herself.

"Miles! It's so nice to see you again. Please, come in," her grandma welcomed, shooting Jules a quick side glance.

Picking up on the warning, Jules added, "Yes, hi. Come in and I'll show you which fans are broken."

Leading him upstairs, she took a moment to collect herself. Miles was only here to fix the fans because he was a nice guy. Not because he still had feelings for her.

He took one look at the ceiling fans and immediately knew what to do. Apparently, he'd just installed a similar fan in his own bedroom. Which was great, except the mention of his bedroom sent her thoughts to his bed, and her in it. Jules promptly excused herself.

Making her way downstairs, Jules caught her grandma standing wobbly in front of the counter with her weight on her good hip, prepping the pesto sauce.

"Excuse me, you're supposed to be seated comfortably in the passenger seat of this kitchen while I drive," Jules called from the doorway. Putting her hands up in mock surrender, Grandma Rosa put down the knife and hobbled over to a chair.

"You know I can't help myself," she said before adding, "Just like you can't help but act a fool around that boy upstairs. You know I can read you like a book, right?"

"You don't know what you're talking about, old lady," said Jules.

"It wouldn't be the worst thing in the world to find your way back to him. Could do you some good, you know."

Slowly turning to face her grandma, Jules said in a low voice, "You know why that can't happen. He has a good life here. He doesn't need me breaking his heart all over again with the truth."

"If I remember correctly, he wasn't the only one with a broken heart."

"No, he wasn't, which is just another reason I can't go there."

"Fair enough," was all Rosa said before dropping the subject. It never did any good to argue with Jules. Plus, her grandma knew everything Jules went through after prom and understood that bringing it up could open old wounds.

The sauce didn't take long to come together in the large pot on the stove while the focaccia baked in the oven, filling the house with the smells of yeasty bread as Jules rolled out the gnocchi and cut them into one-inch pieces for boiling.

Cooking in this kitchen again felt rhythmic and familiar. Like riding a bike again after forgetting it in the garage for a long time. She found herself floating around easily, following her grandma's instructions but also knowing instinctively what to do next with a sense of control that intoxicated her. Tonight, time seemed to bend and slide by without either of them noticing.

After what felt like only mere minutes, Jules looked up at the kitchen door and was startled to see Miles standing there, calmly watching them cook. Flustered at the reminder he was in the house, Jules burned her wrist on the large pot of boiling gnocchi, cursing loudly. *How long had he been standing there?*

"You ok?" Miles rushed over to check.

She shooed him away, more concerned with not over cooking her gnocchi, which would explode if they were left in the hot water too long. Without asking, he grabbed plates from the cupboard and started setting the table. He still knew where everything was, as he'd spent countless hours in her grandma's kitchen as a teenager. It both irked Jules and warmed her heart.

Miles had moved to Riverbend from Chicago at the start of his freshman year. The state had sent him to live with his aunt and her kids since his own mother was in and out of rehab and couldn't hold down a steady job, let alone afford to house them both.

Although not ideal, it was the best of his two options: move in with his aunt or go into the foster care system. Like Jules, he'd never met his father. At least his aunt had agreed to take him on so he could stay in one place for high school, and Miles was close with his cousin Ricky. But after meeting Jules in their freshman year, he spent most of his time at Jules' grandparents' house, which was just down the road from his aunt's. It all seemed to work out right up until everything changed on prom night.

At the dining table, the three of them ate in silence for a few moments, enjoying the rustic yet delectable food. Jules knew she'd done well as she watched Miles and her grandma relish the ritual of breaking bread together. She loved that feeling, the way good food could make people pause and forget their day for a few pleasurable minutes at the table while satisfying the need to nourish their bodies. It felt primal and natural.

Forgetting the awkward tension from before, the conversation eventually flowed freely from Miles' home renovation and the house garden that needed serious attention to the newest true crime podcast Jules was binging. Laughter rose through the kitchen window, punctuating the warm evening for anyone who might walk past. For the first time in a while, Jules could feel her walls coming down, something eroding away the tough exterior she'd built over the past decade.

Jules ventured into more personal territory. "How's your cousin, Ricky?" she asked. Immediately, the air in the room shifted.

"Oh, you know. He's Ricky," replied Miles, avoiding eye contact as he swirled his food around on the plate.

Ricky had been in and out of trouble throughout high school, but Jules had hoped he'd matured within the past decade and gotten his life together. Apparently not. Grandma Rosa, who'd been animated all throughout dinner, was suddenly silent, busying herself with refilling her wine glass.

Weird, Jules thought, but decided to not linger on the subject, quickly pivoting the conversation towards the marching band and their next home game.

After they had washed up and put the leftovers in takeaway containers to take to The Landing, Miles offered to go with her to help carry everything inside. Rosa gave Jules an enthusiastic shake of her head, and Jules accepted his offer.

They loaded the containers into his truck and started the quick ten-minute drive to the retirement home at the edge of town, riding in silence as the city streets and sidewalks gave way to plowed cornfields and long stretches of farmland. The air smelled like summer, sweet and thick but with that hint of manure all Midwest towns had. Normally, Jules didn't like driving with the windows down because it blew her hair into her eyes, but she'd slicked her hair back into a bun at the nape of her neck while in the kitchen, so the breeze was nice on her face. Her feet ached slightly from all the cooking, but she felt the contentment that came with relaxing after a long day of hard work.

"It's been a while since you were last back," Miles said, more as a statement than a question.

Elbow propped in the open window, Jules confirmed, "Not since Grandpa Lou's funeral two years ago."

"I'm so sorry, Jules. I meant to say that the other night. He was a good man, and I know you two were close."

"Thanks. We were."

"Why haven't you been back since? Two years is a long time."

Hesitating, not sure if she should tell Miles the full truth about the visit with Luke, she replied softly, "It was a hard trip for many reasons. I guess I've just been trying to forget about it."

The cab of Mile's truck fell back into silence for a moment before she added, "My ex-fiancé, Luke, came with me. Seeing him here, around my family, made me realize some things about him and we broke up as soon as we got back to D.C."

"That sounds rough," was all Miles said, leaving space for her to continue or change the subject.

Jules hadn't talked about what really happened to anyone. Just gave the simple explanation that they weren't right for each other, which was the truth. But it was more than that, and she didn't know how to put it into words.

"It was, but I'm glad it happened before we actually tied the knot. Saved me many unhappy years and a lot of money."

"Even so, I'm sure it still hurt."

"It did, especially when I realized at the funeral I didn't want him there. It sounds awful, but I had a moment when I looked at him and all I could think was, 'You don't belong here.' It's hard to explain. I don't really understand it myself, but I just knew it wasn't right." She turned towards him, eyes heavy and cast down. "Maybe Grandpa Lou was trying to warn me from the beyond. That'd be just like him to do."

Miles chuckled and continued driving until they pulled into the circular drive of the retirement home. Grandma Rosa must have called ahead because Val was waiting outside to greet them.

"You don't know how happy you're about to make these ladies on their bridge night," joked Val, looking at the food as Jules and Miles carried it into the clubhouse.

She was right, it was bridge night at The Landing and a full table of women wearing their Sunday best rowdily clapped as they set the food down on a nearby buffet.

"I'll be back sometime this week with more," Jules promised Val as she walked them back out.

"You're a good granddaughter. I know Rosa probably doesn't say it often, but boy, howdy, does she love you! You're all she ever talks about. To her, you hang the moon."

Jules' cheeks immediately flared, turning several shades of red. She was never good at receiving compliments. Looking at her feet, she mumbled a swift, "Thanks," before climbing back into the truck.

Back home, Miles insisted on walking her to the door again. The sun was sliding fast behind the horizon, casting long dark shadows across the front lawn. The porch lights were on, welcoming them. At the door, they both lingered, waiting for words to find their way into the night.

Hands in his pockets, Miles looked directly at Jules. "He sounds like a weak man."

"Who?"

"Luke. He should have fought for you. What a stupid man to let you go that easily."

"He wasn't weak or stupid," Jules said in an almost whisper.

"Yes, he was. I'd know. I was, too." Jules' eyes flicked straight up to meet his. They held another long stare, warmth rippling through her body. She could hear her heart beating heavily and his breathing picked up pace.

Closing the space between them, he slid his hand gently up against her cheek, cupping her face in his hand. Instinctively, Jules closed her eyes as she tipped her head back, feeling the warmth of his lips meet hers. At first, the kiss was soft, probing. Neither of them sure. But after a few seconds, she wrapped her arms around his body, pulling him closer until their bodies were pressed against each other and the hesitation faded, leaving only passion and hunger. As the kiss deepened, Jules melted into him, feeling his strong chest muscles against her soft body. He tasted the same as he always had, like mint from the gum he often chewed. The kiss felt so familiar, yet entirely new at the same time; he'd grown into a man since the last time they did this. Time had been a kind teacher.

At the sound of her purse falling from her arm and dropping at her feet, Jules suddenly realized they were still on her grandma's front porch. Pulling back from Miles, the cool air sucker-punched her body as her lips went numb, tingling where his just were.

"I'm sorry," she stumbled, leaning down to grab her purse. "Thanks for fixing the fans and helping me drop off the food."

Jules flung the door open and walked inside without turning back. Miles called her name, but she didn't respond, just climbed the stairs up to her room. She needed to be alone. Needed some space to sort out her thoughts.

Sitting on the edge of her bed, Jules could hear the low rumble of Miles' truck pulling away. Tears welled in her eyes, threatening to spill over for the first time since they laid her grandpa to rest. Although, this time, not entirely out of sadness.

Exhausted but mind racing, she tried to calm herself. Her entire body slumped, heavy like lead. It felt so good to be in his arms again, to feel him fit perfectly against her. For the briefest of moments, when their lips met, her mind stilled. If only she could be honest with him about what she did years ago, maybe he'd forgive her. Or just as likely, he'd never want to kiss her again.

Chapter 7

"Butter or cream cheese on your bagel?" Jules asked Grandma Rosa the next morning.

"Do I look like someone who's watching their weight? I'll take both. But it looks like *you* might need more than a coffee and a bagel to shake those cobwebs loose. Didn't sleep well?"

"I have a lot on my mind."

Jules sat down, avoiding eye contact. If her grandma knew she'd kissed Miles last night, she didn't let on. Jules was grateful. She didn't need to think about it anymore, let alone talk about it.

During the dark depths of the night, she vowed to go against her nature and let things with Miles play out. The last time she tried to control their situation, it didn't turn out so well. She didn't want to make that mistake again. And if the time ever felt right, they'd talk about what really happened on prom night, but it didn't need to be forced. They'd only kissed once since she'd been back; it didn't mean anything.

"What are your plans for today?" asked Grandma Rosa, placing a bagel spread with a double schmear in front of her.

"Grabbing lunch with Mom. Care to join? We're going to that Mexican place you love."

Grandma Rosa shook her head, pursing her lips into a fine line as she refilled her coffee mug. Enough said. Jules dropped the subject.

Flipping her phone over, a text from Winnie popped up:

> *Heard you had a hot date at the old people's home last night ;)*

Word got around fast in Riverbend. Jules tried to suppress a bashful smile. She'd respond later. Maybe Winnie could help her sort through what happened. Talk some sense into her. But first, food and caffeine. Then shower and lunch with Barb. Jules would most definitely need a strong drink after that, and Winnie could always be counted on for a cheap therapy session over a chilled glass of white.

That afternoon, on the drive to meet her mother, Jules gave herself a needed pep talk. It was just lunch. If she kept the conversation neutral and surface-level only, they could avoid drama and keep lunch short.

Pulling up to the restaurant, Jules saw the old Honda already parked in front, which shocked her. They'd always joked that Barb would be late to her own funeral.

The dated yet colorful building had red painted arches over each window and playful colored paper lanterns hanging in the front entrance. Barb sat at a round two-top in the front just behind the hostess desk, chips and salsa already on the table.

"You made it!" she shouted, standing for a hug as Jules walked in.

"Did you think I'd stand you up?" Jules asked, noticing the uniform her mom was wearing. She couldn't tell if they were scrubs or not. *Odd.*

"It might have crossed my mind. I wasn't sure if she'd try to talk you out of it."

"Grandma didn't mind," Jules responded, stretching the truth. "Did you already order?

"No, no. I wanted to wait for you. Do you still like cheese enchiladas? I wasn't sure..." Jules shook her head yes and suggested they split an order while perfunctorily looking at the menu to busy her hands.

"I'd like that," Barb said, voice breaking.

Growing up, they'd come here for dinner sometimes and always shared a plate of cheese enchiladas, beans, and rice, which was enough for the two of them plus leftovers. Jules felt a wave of nostalgia wash over her as she took a long look around the restaurant.

"So, how's Grandma doing? Getting around better?" Barb asked, avoiding eye contact.

"She seems alright, although defiant as ever and not listening to a word I say about staying off her hip."

They exchanged quick updates and fell into a pleasant conversation while they waited for their food.

"Where are you living now?" Jules asked, placing her napkin in her lap. She wanted to know more about the uniform but decided to take it slow. Barb sat up a little straighter, as if she'd prepared for this question.

"In Naperville. I have a tiny one-bedroom condo in a cute complex near the ice arena, if you know where that is."

"I think I remember it," Jules responded as the waiter delivered their order.

"Snuggles loves it. She watches all the kiddos coming and going from the window in our living room that overlooks the parking lot."

"Snuggles?"

"My cat," she said, lips turning up into a genuine smile, the kind that shows all your teeth. "I got her about six months ago. The apartment felt lonely."

Jules almost choked on her enchilada.

"You mean you live alone? No boyfriend?"

"No boyfriend. Just me and Snuggles."

This was news to Jules. All her life, her mom jumped from one relationship to the next. The only time she didn't have a boyfriend was when she was living back home, which never lasted long.

"Wow. So, what are you doing for work, then?" Jules pointed to her uniform.

"I'm working as an assistant in an animal hospital and taking night classes to become a veterinary tech. I'm hoping they'll hire me on full-time after I graduate. I really love it." Barb fiddled with the napkin in her lap.

"That's great, Mom."

Now the uniform made sense, although Jules was stunned that she had stuck with a job for this long. Maybe Grandma Rosa had it wrong this time. Or it could just be another one of Barb's phases. Either way, Jules figured that it didn't hurt to be supportive.

"Anyway, enough about me. Tell me all about D.C. and your job," Barb said, waving her hand in the air.

Jules gave her a quick rundown of her life, realizing there wasn't much to share. She had a simple routine that consisted of work, the gym, and an occasional happy hour or swanky work-related dinner event. She liked the reliable consistency of it all. But from the sound of it, Barb was doing a better job at working towards her dreams and creating a life she loved than Jules.

Their lunch lasted longer than either of them expected. After filling each other in on the current state of their lives, the conversation turned towards Grandma Rosa's fall. Jules knew the broad strokes of what happened, but Rosa refused to talk about it. Barb knew the full story. She was still on Grandma Rosa's emergency contact list, so the hospital had called her when it happened, but Rosa had refused to talk. That's when Val stepped in and kept Barb informed on the side.

Barb shared that Grandma Rosa had hired a landscaping service a few months back to take care of the yard. Mowing, weeding, edging, the things Grandpa Lou always did. On one of their service visits, the lawn mower ran into the wooden birdhouse Grandpa Lou had made in his wood shop years ago, breaking it into pieces.

Hearing the commotion, Grandma Rosa rushed out her front door, upset and ready to raise hell. She lost her footing and fell down the concrete steps, landing on her hip. When the ambulance arrived, her fury had turned to tears. She called Val on the ride to the hospital, sobbing into the phone about the birdhouse. For thirty years, Grandpa Lou had painted and resealed it every summer for the birds to enjoy.

The story broke Jules' heart. She'd never seen her grandma cry. She was always the strong, stoic type. Even at the memorial service, Rosa stood at the end of the receiving line, stone-faced and unflinching the entire time. Of course, Jules knew she was hurting, but it wasn't until now that she understood the extent of her grief. Jules wondered if she'd ever get to experience an enduring love like that.

After paying their bill, the two walked together to their cars.

"Thank you for meeting me today. I know there's a lot left unsaid between us, but I'm hoping we can try to work through it." Barb ran her fingers through her short brown hair. "I want to be in your life, Jules."

Fidgeting with her keys, Jules wavered. She'd heard a version of this so many times over the years, but it never stuck. Barb always went back to prioritizing her wants over everything else, including Jules.

Today, though, felt different. Barb seemed different. Ignoring her instinct, Jules enveloped her mom in a hug. A real hug this time. She wasn't ready to forgive her, but she could start by acknowledging her efforts to be a better person. They'd see where things led.

After their goodbyes, they made tentative plans to see each other again before Jules went back to D.C. at the end of the month.

As she turned into the drive of the old red brick house, Jules' phone rang, which it hadn't done in days. During a normal day, she talked to Becca or the secretary multiple times on the phone if they weren't in person together.

Picking up after two rings, she heard Winnie on the other end.

"Why is Miles texting me, asking for your number? What did I miss over the last forty-eight hours? Are you ignoring my texts?"

Jules sighed. Why did things always get so complicated when she came home? She wasn't used to this type of first-hand interrogation of her personal life, although she could use Winnie's advice.

"Hey there. Can I come over? I'll bring wine."

Being the great friend she is, Winnie agreed before remembering she should check with her partner first. Thankfully, Emily gave an enthusiastic, "Of course! We'll make it a girls' night," in the background.

Jules told them she'd be over after getting her grandma settled for the evening and picking up the promised wine.

Making her way back through the house to the kitchen, she smelled food cooking and knew her grandma was already working on dinner, to Jules' frustration.

"I know, I know, I should be resting," she said, standing at the stove before Jules could say a word. "But my physical therapist also said that I needed to move a few hours a day, so that's what I'm doing."

"Ok, I'll allow it this time. But this better not mean you're kicking me out of the kitchen for the rest of the time I'm here," Jules said. "We still have three weeks together. I need to stay busy!"

"I know someone who could keep you busy, if only you weren't so stubborn," Grandma Rosa said with a tilt of her head.

"Grandma!" Jules exclaimed in horror.

"What? I'm old, not dead. Everyone with decent eyesight can see Miles is fit. Not to mention those muscles. I imagine he would look great without a shirt."

Jules groaned. She hated talking about anything sexual with her grandma. It just felt wrong, but Grandma Rosa didn't seem to care. She always had a bit of a dirty mind.

"I'm going to choose to ignore you said that."

"It's what you're good at."

"Alright, well, since you just want to poke fun at me, I'm going to go to Winnie's and drink some wine. Looks like you have dinner covered. Do you think you can manage the stairs by yourself, Miss Independent?"

Grandma Rosa turned from the pot she was stirring, giving Jules a narrowed look.

"Baby girl, I've been going up and down those stairs by myself since the day after I got back home. I just needed you to feel helpful."

"Wonderful," was all Jules said as she stood to kiss her grandma on the cheek and headed back out towards the car.

"Don't drink and drive," Grandma Rosa shouted after her.

***

Junk food sprawled across the living room table as Jules entered, holding two bottles of wine up like a gift at the altar. They didn't mess around on "girls' night."

Glasses poured, shoes kicked off, and bags of Lays opened, they settled in for a few hours of chit chat and laughs. It felt like the old days when Winnie and Jules would have sleepovers, taking over Winnie's basement for the night and camping out in mounds of comforters with candy and soda always on hand.

"I don't want to be nosey, but tell us everything," said Winnie, popping M&M's into her mouth.

Emily feigned a gasp, hand to her heart. "You, nosey? Never."

"Well, Miles came over the other night," started Jules.

"What?!" yelled Winnie, slapping both hands on her lap and leaning forward.

"Calm down, it was just to help fix the upstairs ceiling fans, and so I could repay him with dinner for the last time he helped with the sink."

"Alright. Not entirely buying it, but go on." Emily patted Winnie's arm to slow her down.

"Well, I promised Val that I'd start bringing leftovers to the retirement village, so he drove me there and helped carry in the containers," Jules continued. At the next part, she paused, feeling somewhat uncomfortable explaining it. She wasn't one to kiss and tell, but she needed to tell someone, and Winnie knew her better than anyone.

"When we got back, he kissed me at the front door," she blurted, looking down into her wine glass as she swirled it around.

"He did what?!"

"Did you kiss him back?" Emily cut in.

Popping a potato chip into her mouth, Jules shook her head yes. "Until I accidentally dropped my bag and came to my senses."

Fixing her face back to neutral, Winnie calmed herself and asked how it made her feel. "Did you like it?"

"I didn't *not* like it. But it's confusing. And I don't want to start anything I can't finish. I'm going back to D.C. in just a few short weeks. That wouldn't be fair to either of us."

"Yeah, I get that. Ever the practical one. But hear me out," said Winnie. "You're both consenting adults now. It doesn't need to be anything serious. You can have fun while you're here and then when you go back, just be friends. No harm, no foul. When was the last time you got laid?"

Emily and Jules both rolled their eyes at that last part.

"That doesn't matter. It's not the point," said Jules.

"Why can't it be the point? You haven't dated anyone since Luke, and you clearly still have chemistry with Miles. It could do you some good to have a little fun. Let loose for once. Then go back to your boring life in D.C. and pretend it never happened. You know, Emily and I were just a fling back in the day!"

"Not the best example, Winnie. We ended up married, remember?" chimed Emily.

"Yeah, yeah. But it was *fun*. That's what Jules needs." Winnie flung her hands up in the air.

"I hear you. It just feels complicated. I don't know if we'd be able to leave it as just that, a fling. I could feel the weight of the past twelve years in just that one kiss."

There was a momentary pause in the conversation before Winnie tilted her head to the slide, concocting an idea.

"What if you didn't think of him as Miles, your high school sweetheart, who broke your heart? What if he was just a guy you met while you were here? Someone you wanted to get to know a little better and maybe have sex with a few times? You don't even have to talk about the past. Keep that off the table and just go for flirty and sexy."

"Yeah, I like that idea," Emily agreed.

Jules took a moment to think it over while she ate more candy and chips. It *could* work. She'd have to get out of her head and stop overanalyzing everything, but maybe it would be good for her. Although he broke her heart, she knew he was safe. He'd never do anything to physically hurt her. Plus, she couldn't stop thinking about what he was like in bed now. If that kiss was any indication, his skills have most certainly leveled up since high school.

"And it would give you something to do besides cook food for old people," teased Emily.

"Hey, I enjoy cooking food for old people!"

"And you're a superb cook. But maybe work on dusting off those cobwebs in your panties while you're at it," Winnie piled on.

Jules told them she'd think about it. Having a fling *could* be fun. She'd just need to keep her head about her and not let old feelings bubble to the surface.

"Why don't you invite him to the Heritage Days Festival on Friday? Winnie and I were planning to go after work. You two could join us. It could be a fun double date thing. Then you can decide if you want to go home with him."

"That sounds reasonable."

Winnie clapped. "Let's text him right now. I have his number."

"Yeah, I meant to ask you earlier why you had his number," Jules asked, narrowing her eyes at Winnie. Obviously, they were friends, which Winnie neglected to mention during their weekly phone calls over the past year. Jules wasn't mad about it, but she felt like people were handling her with kid gloves.

"All teachers at the school are required to have each other's contact information. For safety reasons," Winnie said, brushing it off. "Give me your phone, I'll add him. Then you can send him a text."

And with that, Jules now had Miles' contact information saved in her phone again, almost like it never left. *Funny how things tend to come full circle*, she thought to herself.

Phone back in her possession, her fingers hovered over the blank text screen. Should she ask him? It would set *something* in motion, but just what, she didn't quite know.

With the false bravery that comes from almost two glasses of wine, she went for it. The worst that could happen between them already had years ago.

She took a long look at the draft, deleting the last line right before she hit send; she didn't want to appear desperate. Plus, candied corn was gross.

The rest of the evening flew by as they ate their way through the mound of food, and Jules and Winnie drank the two bottles dry. Jules noticed Emily still had the same glass from when she first arrived.

They talked about upcoming travel plans; Winnie and Emily were taking a trip to Italy next month. Jules shared her lunch date with her mother, and they both encouraged her to give Barb some grace. Emily's mother, who she wasn't close with, passed away unexpectedly last year, so she knew what regret felt like since they never had a great relationship, either.

The night felt cozy and warm, like they were wrapped in a cocoon sitting in the snug living room on a worn but comfortable cornflower blue couch that matched the curtains. Jules hadn't realized how much she'd needed time with her best friend.

Just as Jules' got ready to pack it in for the night and call an Uber, her phone vibrated. It was a text from Miles.

I'd love to. Pick you up around six?

"Is that Miles?" Winnie chirped as she watched Jules try to suppress a grin.

"He's in for Friday," Jules responded, not looking up from the screen. She couldn't trust her face not to betray her even more. *Be chill*, she told herself. *You're a thirty-year-old woman, for God's sake, this isn't high school anymore.*

"Great! We can meet you both there then."

They sorted the details as Jules collected her shoes.

"I can take you home," said Emily. "I haven't been drinking, so no need to call an Uber." An obvious look passed between Winnie and Emily as she said this.

"What's going on?" Jules asked, darting her eyes between them.

"Go ahead, tell her. I know you're dying to," Emily told Winnie, lips pursed in a bashful smile.

Winnie seized the opportunity, blurting, "We've been doing IVF."

"Wow. That's amazing news." Jules wrapped her arms around them for a group hug. She had known Winnie wanted to be a mother someday, and they were at the age when people started families, so she shouldn't have been that surprised.

"But can't you drink when you're doing IVF?" Jules asked, a bit confused.

Pulling back from the hug, Winnie broke out in a huge smile. "We went for a blood test this morning. It was positive."

Emily wrapped her arms around Winnie's waist, pulling her close. They looked so happy in that moment. When they were younger, Winnie would talk about her future kids as if they were a sure thing, but now it was real.

"It's still early, though. We haven't told anyone yet, so please don't share with anyone else," Emily said to temper expectations, although Jules could tell Winnie had high hopes.

No matter what happened, she knew they would be great parents and told them so.

"Now, let's get you home before you turn into a pumpkin," Emily joked, hyper aware of the conversation taking a turn towards the status of her uterus and private bits.

On the ride home, Jules responded to Miles with a quick, *"Sounds good. See you then,"* and told herself to relax. She had to stop thinking about him or else she'd get no sleep tonight.

Chapter 8

Grandma Rosa's recipe cards covered every available surface of her antique wood dining table. There were so many, Jules wondered if they'd ever be able to cook them all, but that wasn't the point. All that mattered was the opportunity to spend time with her grandma.

Not sure how to file them, she took a step back for a collective look at the hundreds of recipes in front of her. Plan forming in her head, she picked out the recipes that interested her the most and plotted them on a calendar hanging in the kitchen. Her organizing included color-coded sections denoting "Lunch, Dinner, Side, or Dessert." Breakfast was Grandma's least favorite meal; there was not a single breakfast dish in the entire box.

Energized by all the sorting, Jules slipped each of the recipes back into the tin, now arranged in neat sections. The thought crossed her mind it might be easier to see everything if she put them in a book format, but that would take too much time. She needed to focus on the promise she had made to her grandma to cook through as much as they could while she was back.

Shouting up the stairs, Jules asked Grandma Rosa if she wanted to go to the grocery store. After her appointment this morning, Rosa's physical therapist gave her the green light to be on her feet more each day. Her hip was healing well, but she needed to move it. A change of scenery wouldn't hurt either, Jules reasoned.

It took a few minutes to get them out the door and into the car, which she had picked up from Winnie's earlier that morning. Flipping the passenger visor down to open the mirror, Grandma Rosa checked her lipstick and pinched her cheeks for color, although she had a full face of makeup on already. She wouldn't be caught dead without looking like she spent an hour getting ready, even if it was just to go to the grocery store.

"You look great," Jules quipped.

"Right. You just never know who'll run into in this small town." Rosa closed the visor and cast her eyes down, picking at the invisible specs on her trousers.

It hadn't occurred to Jules that her grandma might be feeling nervous about her first trip in public since the accident. Rosa always carried an air of independence about her, so it must be hard for her to have to depend on other people. Barb used to joke that Rosa's spine was made of steel. This proved that at least her hip wasn't.

Still, Grandma Rosa didn't complain. She wouldn't grumble or hide away. She'd face the world head-on, like she'd always done. An injury wouldn't prevent her from living her life, and

Jules admired that. She grew up admiring that strength, hoping that some of it would rub off on her.

"You know, I used to go with my father sometimes to Chicago's South Water Market in the early mornings," Grandma Rosa said, staring out the window at the grey day passing by. "He would wake me up around five, while everyone else was still asleep, and we'd sneak out the back door with our canvas tote bags. That's where my love for all things food started."

Jules nodded, encouraging her grandma to continue. She'd never heard this story.

"We'd hop on our bikes and ride the few blocks in the dark. I remember it being so quiet at that time of day. The energy was different, slower in those moments before the day began; the last moments of stillness that few ever saw," Rosa continued, a wistful look on her face. "My dad and I wouldn't say a word the entire ride. It was as if we were both in on a secret, and neither of us felt the need to talk about it. We were just in it."

The image of her grandma as a young girl riding a bike through the residential city streets during the twilight of the morning hours flashed in Jules' mind and she ached for a moment she'd never experience.

"He went almost every morning to sample the fresh produce for the restaurant and place orders. But on the rare days he took me with him, I felt special. It was the only time we'd ever spent alone together."

Rosa was the eldest of three daughters, and Jules' great grandmother divided her time between the house and the restaurant. The two youngest girls took up most of her attention. Rosa helped as needed, but preferred to be in the restaurant, especially as she got older. And her mother didn't hide that she thought it improper for a young lady to work in a kitchen, even though she did the same almost every day. It drove a wedge between them over the years, one that Jules wasn't certain ever dissolved.

As they drove, Grandma Rosa told Jules how her father taught her how to pick out the best and freshest artichokes, eggplants, juicy red and green peppers, and everything else they could find for that day's menu.

"After a while, we made a game of it," she recalled. "I had to guess which pieces of produce were the best at each stand. If I chose correctly, we'd share a warm slice of pandoro sweet bread from one of my dad's favorite purveyors before loading our haul onto the wire bike racks."

Afterwards, she'd follow him to the restaurant and watch as he prepped food for the day. She still remembered the first morning he invited her to help, clasping his hand over hers as she held onto a large chef's knife, barely tall enough to see over the counter. It wasn't long until he trusted her enough to handle the prep by herself, which she did every morning before school.

"The kitchen became my sanctuary. It's where I learned that to be great at anything takes an incredible amount of control and focus. Things many people lack." She looked at Jules. "Things you have in spades."

Jules could see it all unfolding in her mind, and she longed to know more about her grandma's childhood. It seemed so different from her own.

Pulling into the parking lot in front of John's Shoppe, Jules turned the ignition off and sat for a moment while Rosa gathered her things. She'd heard her grandma tell stories about what it was like growing up and working in her father's restaurant, but never anything quite so intimate. Jules had a sense that there was a lot her grandma was leaving out, but didn't know why.

Jules helped her grandma out of the car, gently holding her elbow as she pushed herself upright almost completely on her own. It was clear Rosa didn't need her as much as she'd anticipated, but Jules didn't care. It had been years since they'd spent this much one-on-one time together, so she was grateful. Their relationship had changed in the years since Jules grew from a young girl to a woman. Now, she appreciated her grandma's wisdom and the stories she shared with her in a new way, through the eyes of a woman who'd experienced the ups and downs of life and could relate on a more personal level.

Together, they made their way through the store, gathering all the ingredients needed for that week's menu of recipes. At the produce section, Grandma Rosa shared her some of her father's tricks to identify the best pieces.

"You have enough here for a feast," said Micky, the current owner, as he scanned their items. He inherited the shop a few decades ago from his father, John.

"We're on a mission to cook our way through some old recipes," said Rosa in an upbeat tone Jules hadn't heard in a while.

"I bet they'll be *delish*, especially if they're your recipes," he replied, smiling back at Rosa.

If Jules didn't know any better, those two were flirting. Her head swiveled back and forth, watching them exchange playful banter as they stood in the checkout line. Trying hard to keep her face as neutral as possible, she loaded their items into the bags they brought, not saying a word.

What was happening? No wonder Grandma Rosa seemed preoccupied with her appearance earlier; she had a crush on the shoppe owner, Jules realized to her horror—and maybe delight? She wasn't sure.

That evening, back home in the kitchen, they laid out all the ingredients to make lasagna from scratch, even the pasta. It had been ages since either of them had rolled out fresh pasta dough, and they looked forward to the rhythm of it. Since they were planning to make enough to take leftovers to The Landing, they got started in the early afternoon. It would take a while; making fresh pasta and sauce was a labor of love. The sauce had to simmer in the big pot for at least two hours. Ideally all day, but they'd gotten too late of a start for that. A couple of hours would have to do.

Mixing the flour with eggs, salt, and a dollop of olive oil, Jules formed the dough into four large balls and covered it with plastic wrap to sit for thirty minutes before rolling it out. During the downtime, she helped her grandma open the cans of San Marzano tomatoes, the only kind she would ever consider using, and poured them into the big pasta pot that once belonged to her great-grandfather. She stood close as Rosa added the seasonings and fresh herbs, along with three onions chopped in half, which would simmer in the sauce until the end, when they'd be used to smear on crusty bread as a sort of tomato-y onion confit that Jules loved.

It felt good to have her grandma cooking alongside her now instead of backseat driving from the table. Neither of them noticed the afternoon tick by. It was an easy thing to do in the kitchen, lose sense of time. It wasn't until after they'd rolled and cut the lasagna sheets that they realized it was getting late. They'd need to hurry if they wanted to get the pans of lasagna assembled and in the oven by five. It would take at least an hour to bake in the oven and they were already cutting it close to dinner time for the eager ladies at The Landing.

With an intentional pep in their step, they got all four pans in the oven with no time to spare. Exhausted from the manual labor, they both plopped down at the table. Jules could see the exhaustion on her grandma's face. She'd been on her feet almost all day, by far the most activity in weeks.

"I've got the rest of it. Why don't you head upstairs, and I'll bring you a plate when it's ready?" she offered.

"I won't say no to that," Rosa said, lifting herself from her chair as she reached for the walker.

A pang of guilt flared in Jules. Going forward, she'd be a better caretaker and not let her grandma go that long without sitting again. It was too easy to get caught up in the moment and forget that her grandma was still healing.

Shame tugging at her, she grabbed her phone, in need of a distraction. It was still sitting in her purse, hanging on the back of the chair where it'd been since they'd gotten back home from the store. Forgetting about it was becoming a habit.

Only a few unread emails from her boss, Becca, waited for her. She'd read them more thoroughly later tonight in her room; she still owed Becca a response and signed papers, although it was the last thing she wanted to think about right now. It all seemed so distant. How had only a week and a half gone by? It was as if she'd been here for a year, her memories of D.C. fading into black and white.

Just as she clicked out of her email, the phone lit up with a new text from Miles:

Still on for our date tomorrow?

Does it qualify as a date? Jules wondered. Or was it more of an experiment to test whether they could handle a fling?

Date, huh? Yes, we're still on.

It is a date. See you tomorrow at five. I'll be the one in the convertible.

Convertible? Jules thought he drove a truck. An obnoxious truck. But maybe he had another car? The thought washed over her with relief. She hadn't realized how much the truck bothered her. It just seemed so *not* Miles. So much so that it made her doubt she still knew him at all; maybe their time apart had changed him. She knew the fear was unfair; she'd likely changed in ways that made her unrecognizable to him as well. But, then again, their bodies still responded to each other like they used to.

Before she could over-analyze it, Jules turned her phone to silent and shoved it to the bottom of her purse to keep it out of reach, returning her attention back to the dinner she was making for her grandma and the ladies at The Landing. She didn't want to disappoint this group of posh, opinionated women.

***

The red sports car crawled up the drive right on time, top down. Miles smiled, wavy hair windblown and looking effortlessly sexy in his black V-neck t-shirt and retro Ray-Ban sunglasses. After admiring the view, Jules hopped up from her seat on the front steps where she had been waiting, like she had done many times as a teenager. It all felt too familiar, except for the expensive vintage car picking her up.

"Can I fancy you for a ride to the ball, my dear?" said Miles in an awful English accent. He had always been terrible at accents; time hadn't made that any better.

The sports car looked like a classic, maybe from the '80s, and it was exactly what Jules had pictured Miles driving. Not some large, generic pickup truck. She slid into the white leather passenger seat, pulling her hair back into a loose ponytail to keep it out of her face so she could enjoy the short drive.

A few miles outside of town, they turned off a main road onto a grass and gravel side street which led to the open field where the festival took place each fall. It smelled of fresh-cut grass and damp earth. Off to the right, in an almost hidden clearing, sat an old picnic table Jules had hoped was still there. It looked the same, except maybe a little more weathered by age.

"This will be our place. A special spot we can escape to when life is too much," she heard her Grandpa Lou say, lost in the hazy mist of a faraway memory.

When she was in elementary school, Grandpa Lou had made about a dozen picnic tables in his workshop, which he donated to the local park district to place around town. This table was the very last one he made, so as a surprise, he'd engraved it with Jules' initials. On the weekends, he would pack a basket of bread, cheese, and jam, and they would often have lunch here, overlooking a field of wildflowers and old hardwood trees that buzzed with insects and birds. She loved running her fingers over the carving of initials as they sat and could still feel them as if it were just yesterday.

They passed the picnic table, turning into a makeshift parking lot in front of the festival grounds. It looked like half the town was here, but they got lucky, spotting an empty space where a car had just left.

The Heritage Days Festival had gone on for decades in Riverbend. Taking place in September after school started back up for the year, it ran for three days over a weekend. Jules used to look forward to it every year. Her grandpa would volunteer to role play as a seventeenth-century furniture maker, and she'd spend hours at his side in their booth, watching him dressed in period clothing, talk about woodworking in an old-timey accent she loved.

That's what Heritage Days was all about, celebrating pioneer life. There'd be reenactments of all sorts, from Native American displays of teepees and leather tanning to homesteading pastimes like churning butter and axe throwing. All the sixth-grade classes took a field trip out to Heritage Days on Friday morning, before it opened to the public, to get a private tour of the reenactments and to learn to make bread and soup like they did hundreds of years ago.

Walking up to the ticket booth, they spotted Winnie and Emily already buying their admission and drink tickets. They hurried through the line and collected their first round of "Heritage Hops" beer, made by a local home brewer. Emily opted for a lemonade. Taking a sip, Jules enjoyed the light, crisp taste, surprising herself since it wasn't her usual glass of chilled white wine. The late afternoon air smelled of cut grass and honey wafting in over the trees with a warm breeze. It had rained the day before, so the ground was moist but not enough to cake mud on their shoes. The tall trees loomed above them, still thick with leaves that had not yet turned colors. Everything seemed cleansed, waiting for fall to arrive.

They made their way around the field, stopping at a few of the market stands selling handmade soaps, jewelry, and various housewares which dotted the perimeter of the festival area. Winnie remarked at one point it had morphed into more of an art and craft fair than a festival aimed at recreating seventeenth-century life in the Midwest, but overall, the spirit of the festival still felt alive.

Grabbing Miles by the forearm, Jules led them over to the old log home situated in the middle of the celebration to watch a demonstration on quilt-making from a woman she vaguely recognized.

"Thinking about taking up a new hobby, huh?" Miles asked as they watched.

"You never know. It could come in handy when I leave D.C. to buy a farm and go completely off grid," she joked.

"City slicker you, going off grid? Never."

"I could say the same thing about you coming back to Riverbend. Never thought I'd catch you back here." Jules casted a glance his way but quickly returned her attention back to the woman holding the large multi-colored quilt. He didn't need to know how much she'd wondered what brought him back here.

"For a long time, I didn't think I'd ever come back either. But things changed, and—" was all he got out before a hand clamped down on his shoulder.

A large, burly man stood just behind him, dressed in an intricate-looking costume with a fiddle dangling from his free hand.

"Miles, nice to see you here," he said with a wide smile before coming to a quick stop, eyes resting on Jules.

"Jules Cuccia, is that you?" he bellowed, pulling her in for a tight hug. Jason Fedema was a legend in these parts. For more than three decades, he led the high school band, taking it from obscurity to the powerhouse ensemble it was today.

"Hi, Mr. Fedema. It's great to see you," Jules mumbled into his wide shoulder, delighted to see him.

"Oh, none of that now. It's Jason. I haven't gone by Mr. Fedema since I retired two years ago." He took a deliberate step back, chuckling at himself. "You haven't changed a bit!"

While they both knew that wasn't true, Jason looked like he hadn't aged a day since the last time she saw him twelve years ago. The same salt and pepper curls poked from his head in an unruly way that gave him the air of a distinguished professor with no fashion sense, and his round belly still tested the limits of the buttons on his shirt.

Pushing his metal-framed glasses up his nose, a confused looked crossed his face as he looked between between Miles and Jules.

"Are you two kids back together?"

A long pause hung in the air until Miles held his hand out to Jules in a gesture to explain.

"We're just friends. I'm home to help my grandma, who just had her hip replaced," she said. She could see Miles' jaw clench out of the corner of her eye. *What did he expect her to say?*

"Well, isn't that nice? You should come by the school to see the band practice one day. Miles could use all the help he can get." Jason slapped Miles on the back, adding that he often dropped in as well. Jules logged that for later. She wondered if he was part of the reason Miles came back to Riverbend. The timing lined up.

After a few more minutes of small talk, Jason excused himself to regale others with his fiddle, a crowd forming around him as he played near the candy-apple stand.

The early evening sky took on a purplish and pink hue, like it had been painted in watercolors just for them. Every few minutes, Jules would spot someone she recognized from her childhood, all grown up and with children of their own. It was like she had time hopped from high school to present day. Her life in D.C. felt separate from Riverbend, on a different timeline altogether.

Watching Miles as they walked around, she noted how comfortable he seemed here, smiling and saying quick hellos to many people walking by. He appeared to fit in here in a way that he never had back when they were in high school. Now, he'd found his home, and Jules was only a guest.

She thought about what others must think of her: *Jules, the big city slicker, who had moved away as soon as possible; what was she doing back here? Couldn't handle the pressure?*

The night crawled by, almost as if they were walking through sweet molasses. Soon enough, though, the sun had set and bonfires were ablaze throughout the field, smoke drifting up through the trees, pointing to the stars shining bright above. When they met back up with Winnie and Emily, someone remarked that it felt like a storybook evening, almost too perfect.

"Well, I know how we can fix that," Miles said with a sneaky grin playing on his lips. "I say we head to the Golden Kernel for something stronger."

Jules hadn't even thought about where the rest of the night would take them, but she didn't hate the idea, either. Forgetting that Emily couldn't drink, she gave an enthusiastic, "I'm in."

"Sounds fun, but I think we're going to call it a night. You two should go, though!" Winnie said, taking Emily's hand.

Jules froze. This was turning into more of a date than she expected. The Golden Kernel would lead to more, if she let it. Was she ready for that? Her stomach flipped out of fear and anticipation, giving way to excitement. She *needed* this, she told herself. Keep it casual; nothing more than a fling.

Miles looked at Jules. "What do you say? Care to join me for a nightcap or two?" His voice reverberated low, alluding to more.

A thrill ran through Jules' lower spine. "Sure, let's do it."

Chapter 9

Right, don't over think it, Jules thought to herself as she rolled her eyes at Winnie's abuse of emojis. She'd been this way since middle school, scribbling hearts and smiley faces all over her notebooks. Jules loved how supportive her best friend was about everything, especially this. It made the whole Miles situation feel less serious than it would have otherwise.

Jules shot a quick text back to apologize for ditching them, promising to make it up, before putting her phone away and resigning herself to do what Winnie said: relax and see where the night took her.

Pulling into the gastropub's parking lot, they realized they weren't the only ones looking for something stronger. The place was packed. Miles had to cruise around back to find an open parking spot.

"Is it always this busy?"

"Not usually. Do you want to go somewhere else?" Miles jerked his head to her.

"No, let's go in. It'll be fun." She swallowed her nerves. Tonight might test her, but she was determined to make the most of it, regardless.

The music blared some kind of country song that was popular a few years ago as they stepped through the front entrance. There had to be at least a dozen people on the dance floor performing a line dance she recognized from high school gym class. The bar stools and tables were all full and others stood in groups holding glasses of beer or liquor as they chatted with each other, forming cliques of all sizes.

Jules glanced at Miles. "Should we do a lap to see if anything opens up?"

"I've got a better idea." He took her hand, leading her through the throngs of people, some more rambunctious than others, to the back corner stage. It was empty except for a stool, a round table against the wall, and a mic stand.

"Stay here for a second. I'll be right back," he said, disappearing around the corner through what she thought might be the kitchen doors. A moment later he returned, carrying an identical stool to the one on stage. Setting it down next to its mate, he positioned the small table in front of them.

"There, best table in the house." He held his hand out in a gesture for her to step up on the stage and take a seat.

"Are you sure this is alright?" Jules asked, looking for the host to reprimand them.

"I think Jax and Roxy will give us a pass if I play a song or two tonight."

"But you don't have your guitar." Jules' heart rate jumped at the thought of him singing while she sat next to him on stage. Now she was nervous for a whole other reason.

Sensing she was uncomfortable, Miles folded her hands in his to reassure her. "I keep one here, but why don't we get a drink and some food first? Then we can feel it out."

Food was a good call. They didn't eat much besides popcorn at the festival and her stomach now threatened to make unattractive noises loud enough to be heard over the music and loud conversations happening all around them.

Just then, a very pregnant woman with dark braided hair that reached her waist walked up to the stage, balancing a tray full of plates. Miles jumped up and wrapped her in a big hug, grabbing the large tray from her as Roxy's steel grey eyes landed on Jules. Her skin was a beautiful honey mocha color that contrasted her bright eyes.

"Miles, I didn't know you were coming tonight. And this must be the illusive Jules I've been hearing so much about," she said to them both.

"Sure is. Jules, meet Roxy," Miles introduced as Jules shook Roxy's hand. "We just left the Heritage Days festival. Thought we could use a proper drink and some food."

"It's so nice to finally meet you, Jules. Sorry it's so crowded. Don't be surprised if he ropes you into a duet."

Jules pulled a sour face and laughed. She instantly liked Roxy.

They both ordered a drink with some truffle fries and a goat cheese flatbread to share. Miles said it was his favorite.

"Goat cheese flatbread in Riverbend. Never thought I'd live to see the day," Jules teased.

"You'd be surprised at how much people around here love this place, especially the food. It didn't catch on right away, you know how this town is slow to change," he explained. "But after the *Riverbend Chronicle* ran a feature on the renovations, people gave it a chance. Before Jax and Roxy knew it, they had to hire a full staff just to keep up with demand."

"I'm happy it's working out for them. The tale of the failing restaurant is all too common now days."

"Jax and Roxy are not afraid of failure. Never have been. When I met them in Chicago years ago, they were running a pet spa business out of a warehouse in the commercial district. Did pretty well, too, until they had enough money to buy their own restaurant, which was always Roxy's dream."

Jules was in awe; taking risks wasn't in her nature. Now, though, she couldn't help but wonder what her life might have been like if she'd pursued her passion for cooking and went to culinary school or worked her way up in the restaurant world. Would she be happier or maybe more fulfilled? A heaviness settled in her gut.

"How long have you known them?" she asked, trying to focus back on the conversation.

"Oh, over a decade now, I guess. I met them when I moved back to Chicago after—" he paused, "high school."

"Ah, I see. Sounds like they've been great friends, then."

She didn't want to talk about that period of their lives. Not here, not in this moment at least. Luckily, she didn't need to worry. Right then, Jax showed up with their beers, winking at Jules and saying a quick hello before rushing back to man the busy bar.

After that, the conversation stayed lighthearted as Miles talked about his students and the renovations on his house and Jules told him about her job in D.C. They were enjoying each other's company but steering clear of anything that reminded them of the past. It was a delicate dance, one they were both expertly executing. After all, they had years to catch up on.

Later, the night calmed, and the crowd thinned with the noise level lowering enough that they didn't need to shout over the table anymore. After eating, Jules excused herself to go to the restroom. Strolling back into the main area, a familiar song floated over the speakers. Jules stopped in her tracks.

On stage, Miles sang "Sweet Disposition" by Temper Trap. Even with her nerves dulled by the alcohol, she felt a constricting sensation crawl up her body. She hadn't heard it in years, but she could still recall the first time Miles played it for her. It was after school, on a warm fall day. They were laying in the grass field next to the school, passing time as teenagers do when he placed his headphones over her years and told her to listen. She was mesmerized. The lyrics spoke to her. From then on, she'd always thought of it as theirs. But after prom, it became a hurtful reminder of what she'd lost, and she avoided it at all costs.

Jules' throat constricted as she made eye contact with Miles across the room. He was singing to her, again, and the rest of the room faded into the background. It was happening, again.

For a moment, she felt light-headed. It had been years since she'd been able to listen to this song with anything but a heavy sadness, but now she felt lighter somehow. The lyrics clicked into place when he sang them, like listening to a great song you hadn't heard in a long time that reminded you of a past life.

Jules found an empty chair next to her and sat down without breaking eye contact. They stayed locked together in that moment until the end of the song, when Miles bent around to take a drink of his water. Finally, Jules let out her breath, pressure releasing from her shoulders and neck. She didn't know what to think.

Her pulse racing, Jules couldn't keep her eyes off Miles as he tidied up the stage. She loved seeing him now as a grown man but hearing him sing their song brought back the young man she used to love, the one she'd counted on for four years, right until he'd broken her trust. The rapid switch in perspective left her confused but intrigued to know more about the man he'd grown into. Maybe she'd been too harsh on him all those years ago? It was hard to tell now that they were twelve years removed and all that remained was a haze of unreliable memories.

Jax announced last call as Jules made her way back to the stage, raw emotions still just below the surface. They didn't say anything as Miles packed up his guitar. They didn't need to.

The place was almost empty now, so they relocated to the bar. What looked like a few regulars lingered at the other end, looking to get one last round in before Jax kicked them out. Roxy pulled up another stool.

"Done for the night?" Miles asked, tipping his head to Roxy.

"Heck yes. My ankles are so swollen you can't tell where my feet end and legs begin," she said, looking exhausted.

"You're a trooper. I think I'd be on the floor even if I weren't growing a small child," Jules said with a genuine smile.

Roxy laughed. "Well, this place is like my first child. Very demanding and rarely lets me sleep, yet I still love it."

"I suppose that's true," Jules responded, not knowing what that must feel like.

Roxy turned to Miles. "Speaking of demanding, I was going to ask if you might be free for the Bear Ball in two weeks? It's on Saturday. We could use some help getting ready for it and would love it if you could play a while after the dinner service."

"Of course, I was already planning to attend so I could drum up more donations for the band, but I'd love to play as well. I can even bring a few more musicians for a trio."

The Bear Ball was the school district's annual fundraiser for the arts and music departments and had been a tradition for decades. Each year, the event sponsors tried to outdo the previous year's event, growing it into a swanky gala-style night, even for Riverbend standards. Now, attendees dressed up in suits and long gowns for a fancy dinner and the opportunity to hobnob with the mayor and school superintendent.

Tickets weren't cheap, and this year, the pressure was even more intense to elevate the night because funding for the programs was at a historic low and they needed donations. Miles mentioned that the stakes were high for not only his band but the entire arts program. That's why he had suggested hosting it at the Golden Kernel instead of the community center, which didn't have as much capacity.

Rubbing her belly, Roxy joked she hoped her second child didn't decide to make an early entrance before the big night. There was too much to do and so much food to cook. Jax joined them after the last of the customers had filed out.

Jules sipped a glass of water as they all chatted, filling each other in on their respective evenings. Roxy told them about the couple who were caught hooking up in the men's restroom earlier that night. Turns out their spouses had been waiting for them at the bar when the woman's husband got anxious and walked in on them. Apparently, it caused quite a scene and gave the staff some entertainment for the evening. While they talked, Miles found a reason to touch Jules either on the knee, arm, or squeeze her side when she poked fun at him every few minutes. It was distracting in the best way.

After a while, the conversation shifted to Jules and what she did in D.C., which seemed to fascinate Roxy and Jax, although made Jules feel like an uppity fake in comparison.

"You know, Jules is an excellent cook," Miles quipped, draping his arm over the back of her chair as Jules' cheeks went hot. "She's been cooking with her Italian grandma a lot since she came home, but it's always been in her blood."

"Oh, really? That's wonderful!" Roxy said with a glint in her eye that suggested she was being genuine.

"It's just a hobby I picked up when I was young. My grandma grew up in the restaurant industry. Her father owned a place in Chicago years ago."

"On the north side?" Jax asked.

"I think so. He sold it decades ago, so I never visited."

"That neighborhood has changed so much, but I used to love going to the markets near there. So many more options than what we can get fresh here," Roxy said, twirling her hands in the apron that she'd yet to take off. "It's my one big complaint about living here!"

Jules couldn't help but notice how comfortable they all seemed, like they all belonged. She was beginning to feel at ease, too, drinking the last of her water. After a few more minutes of talk about the gastropub and Roxy's pregnancy woes, Miles and Jules headed towards the door. The night air was crisp, with just a hint of a chill. It felt glorious on Jules' face as she took a large breath to steady herself once outside. Now is when she'd find out where the night would take her: back to the twin bed waiting for her at her grandma's or perhaps another bed?

Feeling unsure of herself, Jules lingered on the front patio, pretending to check her phone to kill some time.

"Is Rosa alright?" Miles asked.

"Oh yes, I'm sure she's fine. She texted about an hour ago saying she was heading to bed." Teenage-like butterflies swept through her stomach, which she hadn't felt in years.

"Well, if you don't have to go back right away, maybe you'd want to come see my new place?" He tilted his head to the side, eyebrows raised in that sexy way of his. So nonchalant but full of meaning.

Jules managed a steady and confident, "Sure. I'd like that," before following him to the car, grateful she at least sounded in control, although her hands trembled in anticipation.

The house looked completely different from the last time she saw it years ago. Gone were the garden gnomes that used to litter the yard. Instead, the luscious grass was neatly manicured, with flower beds full of trimmed bushes and large rocks lining the front entrance. The once-yellow siding had been replaced with clean white wooden slats that contrasted against the black front door and windowpanes. It looked both modern and classical, much like Miles himself.

"Wow, this looks beautiful. You did all of this?" Jules asked, sitting in the driveway, gaping at the house.

"Mostly, but I had some help from people around town. It's still a work in progress, but I'm happy with the way it's turning out. It's finally feeling like mine."

"You should be proud."

"Thanks. I think I am."

Stepping inside the front door, a warm furry animal wrapped itself around Jules' ankles.

"This must be Sir-Toots-A-Lot," she said, bending down to run her hands over his soft fur as he purred.

"The one and only. Though, I'm surprised he's here and not hiding under the couch like he usually does when people come into the house. He must have a good feeling about you," he teased.

Miles gave Jules a quick tour of the house as the cat followed behind. The front living room was tastefully decorated, with modern touches like sleek brass floor lamps and a black leather couch that faced a brick fireplace, with a TV mounted above. A guitar and saxophone case sat next to the sofa. Just off the living room was a well-appointed dining space that opened into an airy kitchen with white and light oak cabinets.

After checking out the guest bedrooms and hall bath, they made their way down to the last door on the right, his bedroom. As soon as Miles pushed the door open, the sweet and musky scent she'd always associated with Miles wafted into the hallway. The room was larger than the others, with an updated bathroom off to the right and a large, hand-carved bedframe holding a king mattress anchored to the middle in front of a row of windows. It felt cozy, although the ceiling soared above. As Jules' eyes swept across the room, she became acutely aware of Miles standing closely behind her, breath warm on her neck.

"This is a nice room," she said in a low voice, frozen in place.

"Thanks." He lightly ran his hand up the back of Jules' arm, closing the distance between them. The hairs on her skin rose at his touch. Every sense seemed to heighten, slowing down time. Wrapping his other hand low around her waist, Miles drew Jules back into him, resting his lips in the crook of her neck.

"Is this alright?" he murmured into her.

"Yes," she whispered back, turning to press the front of her body to his, palms on his chest.

"Good, because I don't want to stop."

He ran his hands up her neck, fingers laced into her hair, cradling her head. Their foreheads rested against one another for a long moment as their breathing grew heavy and in sync. Jules' entire body buzzed with need. She couldn't stop even if she wanted to. The heat coming from him felt so good, she melted into his grasp as his mouth covered hers. The kiss was deep and intense, her body responding without conscious thought. Before she knew it, the backs of her upper thighs pressed against the bed.

Slowly, Miles' hand drew up her side, lifting her shirt. His hand was rough, yet warm and confident, sending a thrill through her lower belly. He stepped back, looking her in the eyes as he lifted the shirt over her head. His eyes, heavy with want, penetrated whatever guards she still had up. Deliberately, Jules ran the tips of her fingers under Miles' shirt, slowly feeling his taut muscles all the way as she lifted the hem and removed it.

For a second, they stood there holding each other's gaze before it became too much, and they collapsed onto the bed in a flurry of gasps and rushed movements to remove the rest of the clothes keeping them apart. Naked and burning with desire, Jules asked Miles to get a condom, which he quickly produced from his nightstand. Rolling it slowly down his large and ready shaft, she knew deep down tonight was inevitable from the moment they laid eyes on each other at the school. It felt more real than anything she'd experienced since they'd last done this, and that scared her.

Miles hesitated above Jules before she felt him fill her, losing herself in the strong and rhythmic movement. Miles expertly pulsed, sending pleasure through her entire body as he whispered in her ear that he'd dreamt about this. Her body tightened around him, increasing their pace.

After a few intense moments, Miles wrapped his right arm under Jules' waist and flipped them around, allowing Jules to straddle him. They stilled for a second before Jules ran her hands over his stomach and up his chiseled chest, never breaking eye contact. She pressed her lips to his wet mouth, enjoying the salty taste, and could feel her nipples rub against his skin. Miles' rough hands clasped on her hips, gently rocking her back and forth until the pleasure became almost unbearable.

As if on cue, they both gave way to a sensation so intense it took their breath. Their bodies pushed together, holding onto to each other in fear of floating away.

Lightheaded and satisfied, they lay side by side, foreheads touching as they waited for their heartbeats to return to normal. For the first time since leaving D.C., the voice inside Jules' head was silent, peace drowning her thoughts.

"That was...," Jules started.

"Amazing?" Miles said, opening his eyes to look at her.

"Yes," she breathed. It was something.

Chapter 10

Miles held Jules close to him under the warm and soft comforter.

"What's your life like in D.C.?"

Jules considered the question, her mind still fuzzy with relaxation. "It's different than life here in Riverbend. Faster and more..." she searched for the right word, "intentional. Everyone is working towards an end game."

"Do you like that?"

Again, Jules paused to think about the question. Her defenses were down, and she was more vulnerable than usual, but she still wanted to be thoughtful in her answer. She shouldn't reveal too much.

"I guess a part of me does. The part of me that enjoys healthy competition. It keeps me on my toes..."

"I feel a 'but' coming," Miles said a few seconds after Jules' answer trailed off.

"But, it can be lonely. Sometimes, I wonder if all the work is worth it. Don't get me wrong, I love writing and creating, but lately I've felt detached from purpose. It's hard to explain." She ducked her chin to her chest under his warm arm.

How could she put it into words when she didn't understand it herself? She'd only started thinking about it in the last few weeks, although she could tell it had been lingering in the back of her mind for some time now. And being here, wrapped in his arms surrounded by his scent, the last thing she wanted to think about was D.C. It felt so far away, memories of it coming in broken and unclear.

"When do you go back?" he asked, stiffening.

"In a couple weeks. I suppose I could go back at any time now. Grandma Rosa seems to get along fine on her own. She doesn't need me like I thought."

"Hmm, maybe she doesn't need you to take care of her physically, but I'm willing to bet she still needs you," he said into her shoulder, kissing it and pulling her tighter.

"You're probably right. But enough about me. What made you come back to Riverbend? Did it have anything to do with Mr. Fedema?" Jules stretched her neck to put a little space between them.

"Yes and no. It was a series of things that led me back."

Miles continued, telling her about the hard years that followed high school graduation. About moving to Chicago with his cousin, Ricky, two days after receiving his diploma in the mail, although leaving out details from prom night.

Jules' heart broke as she learned about him living in a rundown apartment on a questionable side of the city for a few years as his cousin became more and more entangled with an illegal drug operation. At first, it was just selling weed here and there, which Miles even took part in to make some extra cash to supplement his meager income as a pizza deliveryman, but it got out of control.

"It was a low point in my life. I never thought about the future. College seemed like a thing that was for other people, not me, a broken, hopeless young man with no prospects and a criminal record," he lamented.

"Did you stop playing music?"

"Not right away. Eventually I sold my instruments for the cash. By then, it didn't even matter. I was bouncing from job to job, just trying to get by. I'd lost myself, and Ricky was the only person who'd stuck around. I tried my best to keep him at arm's length, because I knew what he was involved in. But it was hard, the Miles you used to know was gone," he said, voice cracking with a pained look pinching his face.

"And then, a few years in, Ricky got busted in a massive sting operation. Turned out he was selling more than just weed. It was bad, and he's still in jail. He will be for a long time. When it happened, I even felt guilty for not being with him. I thought maybe I could have done something to prevent it."

He took a deep steadying breath. "But it ultimately served as a wake-up call. It was Roxy and Jax who convinced me to get out of the city. They knew some friends up in Michigan who had a place for rent and could get me a job as a late-night truck driver, so that's what I did."

Jules didn't know what to say. Never in her wildest dreams did she think it could have been this bad for him. While she was heartbroken and in a dark place during that time, she was also living in a safe college dorm, going to classes and learning, not worrying about making rent or being caught up in something illegal. It seemed too unreal to fathom.

"Oh Miles, I'm so sorry you went through that," was all she could say, pulling him closer.

"It feels like another life altogether now. And I'm grateful it happened when it did. It allowed me another shot at building something decent and stable."

Jules felt so much adoration for this man who could now look back on a time like that and see the good in it. It reminded her of the kind soul she fell in love with years ago.

"For a few years, I just worked and slept, saving up money. I didn't know what for, until I started playing guitar again. After that, I knew I wanted to go back to school. But since I was older, I needed a written recommendation to apply, so I reached out to Jason on a whim, not expecting him to respond."

"That's how you got in?"

Miles laughed. "Not quite. Jason called me one day and put me through the wringer a bit. I guess I deserved it. But after that conversation, he agreed to write a recommendation and even call the department chair at the school I was applying to. I think he always hoped that I'd turn my life around."

"That's remarkable, Miles."

"It wasn't easy, but it got easier after that. Jason helped me through it, taking early morning phone calls to talk me through some of my assignments and give me encouragement when I needed it, which was often. He's the reason I pursued a degree in music education after all. I owe so much to him."

Now it all made sense. Jason must have asked him to take over once he retired and Miles couldn't turn him down after all he'd done for him. That had to have been why he moved back to Riverbend. Jason saw the potential in Miles. No way he would have turned the reins over to someone he didn't have full confidence in.

"I'm sure he's just as grateful for you. I don't think Mr. Fedema would have let just anyone lead his band. You must be quite the instructor, Mr. Greene," she teased, playfully running her hand down his torso.

"I could show you if you'd like," he growled, cupping her breast as he wrapped his leg around her. Jules certainly wanted to be taught.

***

Early the next morning, just as the sun rose over the treetops, Miles dropped Jules back at the house and she tiptoed inside, hoping not to wake her grandma before she could change and claim probable deniability that she'd stayed over at Miles'. Although she didn't feel guilty about it, she also didn't feel like discussing her sex life with her grandma, especially because it felt like so much more than just sex. As she climbed the stairs, a stupid grin plastered on her face, she reminded herself to take it slow. This was no time to get wrapped up in anything serious. *Don't catch feelings,* she reminded herself.

She quickly changed out of her clothes from last night, throwing on an easy yellow sundress that made her feel like she should frolic in a field. It matched the way she felt inside. Making her way back down to the kitchen for coffee, she knew she was a fool for thinking she could get anything past Grandma Rosa, who sat there with a smug smile.

"Have fun?"

Not turning to face her, Jules grabbed a mug from the cabinet and filled it with warm coffee from the pot her grandma had brewed.

"It was a perfectly pleasant night."

"That's not the swagger of a woman who just had a 'pleasant' night."

"Since when do you use words like 'swagger'?" Jules asked, trying to change the subject.

"Oh honey, my generation invented swagger, don't flatter yourself. Are you planning to see more of Miles while you're here? Looks like it's doing you some good."

"Maybe, but it's not serious. Don't get too excited. We're just having a bit of fun while I'm here. Nothing more than that," Jules explained, more to herself than to Rosa. She'd have to work on reminding herself, and him, of that if they were to see each other again. It would be too easy to get hurt again.

***

The following week, Jules cooked non-stop, taking food to the retirement community with Grandma Rosa's friend Val almost every night. She was working her way through the recipes she'd organized a few days earlier and gaining more confidence in her cooking skills each meal.

After a while, Jules suggested tweaks and additions to her grandma's recipes. To her surprise, Rosa encouraged her edits. It gave Jules the opportunity to hone her skills, making unique pasta sauces and sensing when and how to use anchovies to deepen a dish's flavor profile. It felt like her own personal culinary school right there in her grandma's familiar and well-loved kitchen.

While the mornings and afternoons flew by cooking and sharing stories with her grandma, Jules tried to make the evenings last as long as possible.

After that first night with Miles, he'd fallen into the habit of texting her each afternoon to see if she was free for the evening. Jules liked how he seemed nervous each time, making him hard to resist, even though she knew they were playing with fire. She found herself spending every night at Miles' after she'd made sure her grandma settled in for the evening.

The pattern went like this: Miles picked her up around eight. They'd go back to his house, he'd play some music and inevitably, they'd make their way to his bed, forcing

Sir-Toots-A-Lot to scratch at the closed door. Not much talking happened while they were together, which suited Jules just fine. Surface-level was all she could handle, and Miles somehow knew that. The time never felt right to bring up their past and she accepted that, grateful to not revisit painful memories.

Every so often, her thoughts would wander to the future and where this was leading, but the relentless cooking during the day kept her focused.

Thankfully, her grandma didn't bring up the topic, either. She just nodded to her as she said goodbye each night, which was encouragement in itself. Rosa wasn't known to stay quiet if she thought you were making a mistake.

For the first time in her adult life, Jules didn't have her next move plotted and planned. She was living in the moment, enjoying the short reprieve from what she considered her real life back in D.C.

"You're...glowing. Is it all the sex you're having?" Winnie even asked at one point.

"Wouldn't you like to know?" She didn't like to kiss and tell, but Winnie had a point. The sex was doing her some good.

They'd also been spending more time together, more in those two weeks than they had in the past five years combined. Almost every morning, Jules joined Winnie at the high school to help with play rehearsals. She couldn't say the cast was good, but they certainly worked hard. But it didn't matter. Jules enjoyed being around people who understood the compulsion to make art for the sake of it. It roused a part of her that had been suppressed for a long time.

About a week into her new routine, while stuffing artichokes with her grandma, her phone chimed with the tone reserved for her boss, Becca. Wiping her hands on the baby blue apron that her grandma had found for her in the back of the pantry, she tapped the screen.

Call me when you get this. Thx!

Jules groaned. She still owed Becca the signed papers for her new role, and she probably wanted to know what the holdup was. Too bad Jules didn't know why she hadn't signed them, either.

Excusing herself from the kitchen, she hurried to her room and closed the door behind her. She didn't want to have this conversation in front of her grandma. Steeling her nerves for the awkwardness sure to follow, Jules hit the call button. There was no use delaying it. To her surprise and disappointment, Becca picked up on the first ring. A part of Jules hoped it would go to voicemail.

"Jules! Thank God you called back." Becca sounded frazzled. Maybe this wasn't about the papers after all.

"Hey, what's going on? Everything alright?" she asked, taking a seat on the edge of her bed.

"Yes, yes, only Secretary Monahan needs to give testimony at a Senate hearing on Friday and wants you to work with him on his remarks and be there at the Capitol."

"This Friday? As in two days from now?" Jules responded, doing some mental math.

"I know I promised not to bother you, but he specifically asked for you." Becca lowered her voice. "Between you and me, he's a bit rattled by the request to testify. It was very unexpected. If you catch a morning flight tomorrow, that will leave you plenty of time to work with him all day before Friday's hearing. I wouldn't ask if it wasn't important."

"Right, I know. I just—" Jules said, catching herself. *She just what? Couldn't come because she'd miss having sex with her high school sweetheart? Or because a few ladies at a retirement home were looking forward to her cooking?* "Never mind. I'll book the first flight out tomorrow."

After their conversation, Jules sat in her room, paralyzed by the thought of packing, leaving her grandma, and losing a few days with her friends. Even though she knew Grandma Rosa would be fine on her own with Val checking up on her, Jules had zero motivation to step back into her real life right now.

Allowing herself to sit with the news, Jules took a few deep breaths to steady her thoughts and gather the energy this would require before grabbing her suitcase to fill it for a quick trip. She'd fly back Saturday on the earliest flight she could get.

That night, after explaining the situation to her grandma and a quick phone call to Winnie, Jules relaxed next to Miles on his couch as he strummed his guitar. He looked so at ease with it in his hands, she allowed herself to melt back into the comfortable cushions, taking in the sexy sight. He had grown an affection for tight-fitting V-neck t-shirts, and she could see why. They showed just the right amount of his chest without looking like an extra on *The Jersey Shore*. Her mouth went dry at the thought of running her hands underneath it later, just before taking it off.

"Am I boring you?" he asked, lifting his eyes to hers.

"Quite the opposite," Jules said, meeting his gaze. "I don't know how any of your students concentrate when they have you to look at." He rolled his eyes and laughed, playing louder.

Although she enjoyed listening to him play, she found herself trapped in her thoughts. The topic of her trip to D.C. hadn't come up yet, and she didn't know why she'd put it off. Miles needed to know, or else he might feel blindsided again, which was the last thing Jules wanted.

During a lull in his strumming, Jules finally mustered the words she needed, "Miles, I got a call from my boss earlier. They need me to go back for a few days." He stopped strumming the guitar, jerking his head up to look at her.

Chapter 11

"But you're coming back, though?" he said, eyes scanning her face.

"Yes, on Saturday. I'm on the first flight out tomorrow."

"Wow, tomorrow? That's quick." He swallowed hard before continuing, "Do you have a ride to the airport?" Although his voice was neutral, it was clear from the strained look on his face that he didn't want her to leave.

"I've arranged a car service to pick me up, since it's so early."

Miles nodded and went back to playing. The feeling in the air had somehow shifted, like the bubble they'd been living in for the past week had burst from the sharp poke of reality. Jules didn't live in Riverbend and would be gone again in a few short weeks. Those were just the facts.

Later that night, after they'd made their way to his bedroom and were lying wrapped around each other, Miles whispered, "I'll miss you."

Jules stiffened under his embrace. She knew she'd miss him too, but they shouldn't say those things out loud. A ringing started in her ears that grew too loud to ignore. This was a mistake; she should have never let it get this far. How could she have thought this would just be a fling with Miles? Of all people, *Miles*?

Quickly, she slid out of the bed and gathered her clothes, pulling them on without so much as a glance at Miles who didn't say a word. Slipping on her white sneakers she looked over her shoulder at the bed, face cast downward.

"I'm sorry. This might have been a mistake."

She gave a small shake of her head and walked out the door, not stopping even after Miles called her name. Once in the driveway, she remembered Miles had picked her up earlier. Through blurry tears, she tapped the Uber app on her phone to order a ride home.

Jules knew Miles deserved an explanation and she should go back inside, but fear kept her rooted in place. She couldn't let herself get hurt again. Couldn't let herself hurt *him* again. Even if she was taking the coward's way out. Better to leave now, than let it go any farther.

***

The airport was quiet the next morning. Only a few people in suits sat waiting for their routine flights to who knew where. Thankfully, Jules had cut it close this time, avoiding the empty downtime she usually experienced before a flight, leaving her just twenty minutes to grab coffee and a bagel before boarding. She'd get caught up on the hearing details on the plane so they could hit the ground running when she got to the secretary's office later. No time to even stop at her apartment; she'd bring her bags with her.

Laying in bed awake the previous night, Jules tried to calm her mind but ended up on a roundabout of thoughts and scenarios. Close to the time she had to get up for her ride to the airport, she swore to herself she'd put all thoughts of Miles and Riverbend out of her mind for the next two days and focus only on the work ahead of her. Becca had given her an opportunity to reconnect with her real life, and that's what she intended to do. Maybe after this trip, she'd be ready to go back to D.C. for good, recommitted to her career and rebuilding the personal life that she'd put on hold for far too long after the split with Luke. She owed it to herself to try again; it was the life she had worked so hard to create.

Rejuvenated with a sense of purpose, Jules strode into the secretary's suite of offices a few hours later. Becca was already waiting to greet her, worry etched across her face. After a quick greeting, Jules headed towards her office to drop her bags before seeing Secretary Monahan.

"So, as you probably suspected, he's anxious to say the least," Becca said, leaning casually against Jules' office door, although her face was tight with worry. Secretary Monahan never liked to be unprepared or surprised, which this last-minute request to testify must feel like to him, although it came with the territory.

"I'm sure he is, but we already have prepared talking points for this exact topic in one of our briefing books. He'll be fine.

He just needs to get comfortable," Jules said as she gathered her notebook and pen out of her tote bag. "Is he ready to start now?"

"Yes, I've cleared his calendar, so we'll have all day to get him ready."

"Perfect. Let's do it."

For the next eight hours, Becca, Jules, and Secretary Monahan holed up in his palatial corner office surrounded by soaring views of the Potomac River. By any standards, it was a beautiful space, even more so because it was in a government-owned building which were often outdated. None of them paid any attention to the view, however, as they poured themselves over binders full of talking points and data. This process was never straightforward, but Jules had learned how to deal with the secretary and his insecurities over the last two years by letting him take his time with the materials. He always came around to some sort of agreement with her recommendations, so long as he felt like he had a say in making them himself.

While they waited for their ordered dinner to arrive, Jules snuck out for a quick break, needing some fresh air. As she rode the elevator down to the bottom floor, she had a moment to reflect, feeling detached and exhausted. Normally, this kind of day was what she lived for, thriving on the chaos of a task with a looming deadline. She worked best under pressure, but now all she could think about was home, although the "home" she pictured in her head wasn't her empty apartment. It was Riverbend.

Startled at the thought, she began aggressively pressing the "lobby" button repeatedly, as if it would make it go any faster. Once outside, Jules regained her composure and breathed in the evening air. Becca joined her after a few moments to indulge in her one vice that not too many people knew about, the occasional Marlboro Light.

"Thanks for coming back. You did great in there," she said, lighting the cigarette. And for a moment, Jules felt glad she was here. Words of affirmation had always meant a lot to her, even if she never learned how to take a compliment. But then she caught an unmistakable edge in Becca's voice when she said, "He was so worried all last night. Poor guy couldn't get an ounce of sleep. He was restless. He just wanted *you*."

Becca turned her head, one arm across her chest, propping the other holding the cigarette to her lips. Her gaze shot a note of warning that Jules had never seen from Becca before.

What was she trying to say? How did she know the secretary couldn't sleep last night, and why did it seem to bother her that he'd requested her help?

Then, as Becca stubbed out her cigarette on the bottom of her heel, Jules was hit with a sense of clarity so forceful it rendered her mute. How stupid and naïve could she have been? They were sleeping together. Of course, they were. It had been right in front of her all along. The way she always seemed to show up to the office mere minutes after he did, their long, closed-door meetings in the middle of the day, and the inside information Becca seemed to always have on his personal life.

Jules thought about the secretary's family. She'd met his wife multiple times, who was lovely, always remembering Jules' name. And the kids were still so young. Not even in high school yet.

Logistically, the affair made sense, though. His family lived in Delaware, and he only went home on the weekends. How had she missed it? Her head swam with memories from the last few years, flicking through the evidence.

By the time Jules found her voice again, Becca was already heading back into the building.

After the initial shock wore off, Jules found she wasn't all too surprised. Maybe that's why she'd kept Becca at arm's length for so long? Maybe, deep down, she knew Becca might be capable of being a part of a betrayal like this.

Luckily, she didn't have to fake ignorance of her newly gained knowledge for too long. The work session ended soon after dinner arrived. On her way out, Jules couldn't help but notice Becca still in her office, waiting for him.

***

Jules unlocked her apartment door, swinging it wide open as a wave of cool air hit her face. She must have forgotten to turn down the air conditioner when she left a few weeks ago. At least the place didn't smell stale, she told herself.

Flicking on the lights, she looked around her apartment. It was clean and modern with tall ceilings held up by walls of windows on two sides. The D.C. night gleamed back at Jules, all warm lights and shadows from the row houses below. A large living room stretched in front of her with two white couches she rarely sat on. To the left was an open-concept kitchen that boasted high-end appliances and an island with room for eight seats. When she'd first toured this place, she fell in love with how open and airy it seemed. Now, the sleek luxury furnishings made her recoil and miss the cozy imperfectness of her grandma's house and the personality Miles brought to his.

Too exhausted to linger on the thought, she took a quick shower to wash the day off before crawling into bed.

Friday started early, with the hearing at eight o'clock and finishing before noon. The secretary did a fine job answering the committee's questions and evading the topics he knew were tricky. For three hours, Jules sat directly behind him, giving him confidence as he knew he could turn and ask for her counsel, which he did twice. Becca sat ramrod straight next to him, hair twisted into a tight bun as she always wore it. Jules wondered if anyone else knew of their affair and had scanned the rotunda for any signs, but everyone seemed oblivious. To the unsuspecting eye, Becca must have looked every part the professional colleague Jules thought she used to be until last night. *How could Becca have allowed herself this enormous lapse of judgment?* Jules couldn't help but feel betrayed, not only on the secretary's family's behalf, but also for herself. Their affair could put Becca and Jules' careers at risk if she joined the new PR firm. Not to mention, it was a bit of a Washington cliché.

Before leaving the Capitol building, the three of them gathered in the hallway.

"Thank you for being here, Jules. I know it cut into time with your family, so I appreciate it," the secretary said, looking relieved to be done.

"Happy to help," was all Jules could say back. She was having a hard time regarding him with the same deference she used to. Becca followed her down the hall as she left, catching her by the arm as they turned the corner.

"Can we grab drinks tonight? I'd like to talk to you," she said, smoothing her black designer shift dress and keeping her voice low. Jules hesitated. She did not want to spend more time with Becca than necessary, but it would give her the opportunity to tell her she wasn't accepting her job offer as chief communications officer. She decided last night to turn it down. Jules didn't know what would come next, but she knew she had to follow her gut on this; she couldn't go into business with someone who would let their personal life become a liability of that magnitude.

"Sure. Just text me when and where," Jules replied and strode down the hall before Becca could say anything else.

In the hours that passed between arriving back at her apartment and meeting with Becca, Jules mulled over the events of the last few days. Her emotions swung back and forth like an out-of-control pendulum. One moment she felt confident in her decision to walk out on Miles, putting an end to their dangerous fling, and the next she felt despondent over the revelation that her life in D.C. might not be her endgame, and with that, her resolution to keep away from Miles eroded. Not for the first time, she was unmoored; it gave her a headache.

Only one thing felt concrete: she would not join Becca's new firm. She'd remain cordial and professional with her, as she was sure their paths would cross again. D.C. was a small town, after all. Jules couldn't shake the feeling of distrust that now clouded her perception of Becca. She wasn't conservative in her own personal beliefs, but Jules drew the line at complicit cheating. It said all it needed to about one's character and she was grateful to have found out before signing the employment contract.

Before exiting the taxi in front of an opulent social club which had recently opened just across the street from the White House, she took a glance at her phone. No messages from Miles. *Probably for the best*, she thought. Jules arched her head back to look up at the tall building and drew in a long steadying breath to ready herself for the conversation ahead with Becca. She was no stranger to confrontation, but she didn't revel in it.

Chapter 12

"Thanks for meeting me here, Jules," Becca said, drawing out her name with a posh tone as Jules approached the empty seat next to her at the long bar. The club was almost empty, even though it was a Friday night.

She took in the beautifully carved wooden bar that wrapped around at both ends, decorated with expensive-looking gold leaf and mirrored accents. Behind them, tables with low, comfortable seating dotted the large room. The club looked like a cross between a scene from *The Great Gatsby* and a Frank Lloyd Wright home. She couldn't tell if she was impressed or confused. Either way, she wasn't planning to stay long. Just enough to have a drink over what would be an uncomfortable conversation.

"This place is...large," Jules said, sliding onto the bar stool.

"Over twenty thousand square feet, I'm told. Being a member has its perks, but I have yet to see all of it."

Becca's hand trembled slightly as she sipped her chilled martini. She was used to having the upper hand in most conversations, but this time was different. Becca had made a misstep by revealing her relationship with the secretary, and they both knew it.

The bartender approached as Jules got settled. The service was better when you paid a premium to even enter. She ordered a French 75, not wanting to seem unrefined with her usual order of the driest Sauvignon Blanc they had on hand. As she waited for her drink, a deafening silence stretched between them. At last, drink in hand, Jules broke the tension.

"How did Secretary Monahan feel about his testimony today?"

Visibly relieved at the softball question, Becca quickly answered with a lift in her voice, "Oh, he was pleased, although I don't think he's eager to do it again anytime soon. Thank you again for coming back on such short notice. We wouldn't have been able to pull it off without you."

"I think you two would have managed just fine together," Jules snipped, looking straight ahead.

"I shouldn't have been jealous that he wanted you there this week. I'm sorry for that. I could blame it on exhaustion, but it was only insecurity." Becca angled her shoulders to face Jules. "It's not easy, you know, keeping it a secret. But honestly, I thought maybe you had already suspected."

"That you were sleeping with the secretary?" Jules blurted. "No, I had not thought that. But looking back, I guess there were signs."

Becca recoiled at her bluntness, looking over her shoulders to ensure no one had overheard her.

"We're not just sleeping together. That makes it sound dirty and scandalous. We have plans to be together publicly soon."

"Does he know you are planning to leave the department and start your firm?"

Jules wasn't interested in hearing any justification for their affair, but a part of her felt sorry for Becca. She was clearly being manipulated.

"Yes, he's helping me finance it and will join as part owner after he finishes his appointment."

"Why did you tell me he didn't know, then?"

"Because of the optics. We can't have people knowing before we go public with our relationship. And that won't happen until he leaves his wife, after he's no longer holding a Cabinet position." Her voice was barely a whisper.

"Sounds pretty scandalous to me. And risky."

Out of the periphery of her vision, Jules saw someone squeeze between the chairs beside her to order a drink.

"We have it all planned out in an iron-clad contract. You don't need to worry. But I will answer any questions you have. I still want you to join the firm, Jules," Becca said, with a pleading look.

At the sound of her name, Jules felt a hand grab her shoulder.

"Jules? I thought it might be you," she heard someone say behind her. She turned and was shocked to see Luke towering over the bar.

"Luke, so nice to see you," Becca purred before Jules could react. Luke lifted his gaze from Jules.

"Oh hi, Becca. Nice to see you as well."

"I would introduce you to my colleague, Jules, but it seems you already know each other?"

Just then, Jules' voice caught up with her. "Yes, we used to be friends."

"We were more than friends, Jules. We were engaged a few years ago," Luke added, tilting his head down at Jules with a mischievous smirk. Oh, how she remembered that look. It made her stomach go sour. It was the same look he gave her when they first met, except then she didn't know any better. Now it only reminded her of his fake charisma.

Becca's lips parted in surprise.

"It didn't work out in the end, though," he added, eyes locked on Jules.

She took in his designer suit and Cartier watch. Luke had always dressed well, but he seemed louder about it now, more brash in his ostentatiousness. He ran a hand through his perfectly coifed dirty blonde hair and asked what she was doing here.

"Just here to meet Becca for a quick drink before calling it a night."

"Right...you're a new member," he said to Becca.

"Joined a few weeks ago and enjoying it so far," she responded, trying to keep his attention.

Luke worked in venture capital, not that Jules understood what he did in that industry. He ran with an exclusive crowd in D.C. and frequently traveled for business to California and abroad. Jules wasn't surprised that Becca knew him.

"You're a part owner, correct?" she asked.

Luke nodded, one hand in his pocket as he sipped his whiskey.

"Do you mind if I steal Jules away for a moment? I'd like to give her a tour of the place and catch up," he asked, looking back at Jules.

"Oh, s—sure," Becca stammered.

"I wasn't planning to stay long," Jules said, not wanting to be alone with Luke. This was not on her bingo card for the day.

"Please, it'll only take a few minutes."

"I can wait for you, Jules," Becca cut in.

The next thing she knew, Jules was walking through the large ornate room, avoiding Luke's hand as he tried to place it on her lower back. Once they'd cleared the main room, Luke going on about the Swedish architect they'd hired to design the place, they stepped into a smaller, more intimate dining area with a modest bar in the corner. It was empty except for one bored-looking bartender.

"It's been, what, two years since we saw each other?" he said, motioning for her to take a seat near a large window.

"Give or take. I haven't been keeping track, honestly."

"You look...well. Different. I like the dark hair."

"Thanks? I'm not sure how to respond to that." She was wary of him and was too tired to hide it.

"I'm surprised to see you here. Not really your scene. But I'm glad we ran into each other," he said before pausing. "What have you been up to?"

Jules didn't know what came over her as she let out a bitter laugh. It could have been the way he asked the question, like she was being interviewed. She'd witnessed him do this to others in the past, sizing them up to gauge their value or his perceived "worthiness."

"I've been away on travel the past few weeks. I'm leaving again tomorrow," she said, offering no details. His eyebrows shot up to his hairline in interest.

"Still at the Treasury Department, though?"

"Yes, but not for much longer," Jules said, surprising herself. As soon as the admission left her lips, she knew it was true. She couldn't work any longer for either Becca or the secretary. What *exactly* she would do next, though, she had no clue.

"Well, that's great to hear. I always thought that job was beneath you."

Taken aback, she screwed her face into a bewildered glare. "I stopped caring what you thought about me a long time ago, Luke."

She couldn't believe she almost married this narcissistic man. No wonder he did so well in D.C. The town was overrun with people just like him. Or at least, that's all she seemed to find herself surrounded by.

When she'd brought Luke home two years ago for her grandfather's funeral, he'd acted as if Riverbend and her family were beneath him. The entire trip, he kept throwing out veiled insults like, "I bet there are more cows here than people." When he found out they would be staying at her grandparents' house, he flat out refused and booked them a room at a fancy bed and breakfast in the town over. He never once took the time to console or even talk to her family members, including her grandma. The last straw was at the funeral when he'd walked off to take a work call and never returned, sitting in the rental car for the entire program.

"No need to get hostile, Jules. You're the one who left me, remember? But I'd be lying if I said I hadn't thought about you since then," he whispered as he leaned in to place his hand on her knee.

For the briefest of moments, Jules considered what her life would have been like if she'd married him. This kind of day would be normal; they'd spend their downtime at clubs and fancy restaurants, pretending to be people they weren't and trying to impress others to drown their disappointment in each other. The vision terrified her.

Standing to go, Jules said, "Nice seeing you again, Luke. I wish you the very best." And with that, she strode back out, leaving Luke sitting alone at the table, speechless.

As she made her way through the main room to where Becca still sat at the bar, she decided her time here was over. There wasn't much left to say but the truth.

Jules collected her things from the stool and turned to Becca, forcing herself to look her in the eyes when she said, "I won't be joining you at the new firm. In fact, you can take this as my resignation from the department as well. All the best to you and the secretary. I hope you know what you're doing."

Becca's mouth fell open, speechless as her cheeks turned a bright red, probably from anger and a healthy dose of embarrassment. Jules didn't plan to stick around to hear what she had to say or to be talked out of it, so she nodded to herself and walked straight to the exit, head high.

It wasn't until Jules was in the taxi riding back to her apartment that it hit her.

She'd quit.

She'd done it. Although the thought had been idly bouncing around her head for some time now, she had never given it any true attention until now, in the heat of the moment. But she calmed her rising panic by reassuring herself she had enough in savings to last almost a year. She'd figure out her next move by then, right? If the last few weeks had taught her anything, it was that her life didn't need to be planned out to the minute. She *could* be happy living with the unknown for a while.

As she watched the streets of the city zip by through the window, a weight lifted off her shoulders for the first time since she arrived in D.C. Whether from her decision to quit her job or getting closure on her relationship with Luke, she didn't care. She was just grateful for those in her life who would help her through the era of the unknown: Grandma Rosa, Winnie, and Miles—*no, not Miles*, she quickly corrected herself. Jules didn't have a claim over him, and it wouldn't be fair to lead him on when everything was up in the air. They hadn't even talked about what came next, if they'd stay in each other's lives beyond her time in Riverbend. Plus, she wasn't sure she'd ever be able to tell him what happened after prom. He was building a steady, quiet life. He didn't need anything messy.

The resolve to put an end to whatever it was they were doing back in Riverbend strengthened as she mulled over her new sense of freedom. Jules texted Winnie to confirm their plans for tomorrow:

> Still planning to pick me up at the airport tomorrow? I can't wait to tell you about how I imploded my life today :)

> Ohh, do tell! Yes, I'll be there tomorrow bright and early. Can't wait to hear all about it <3 Unless you want to talk now?

> No, thanks. I'm good. Just need some sleep and I'll be right as rain. See you soon!

Morning came too soon after a night of fitful sleep that caused Jules to almost miss her alarm. She threw her clothes back in her bag and gave her dying plants another healthy glug of water, making it out in record time. But as she wheeled the suitcase out of the large metal front door, she paused to look back at the beautiful, sophisticated apartment she used to love and let out a long sigh. Things already felt different, and she caught herself wondering if she'd ever see the place with the same affection she once had.

A few minutes later, she was back at the D.C. airport, boarding another plane to Illinois and to the rest of her life, wherever that would take her.

On the flight, Jules didn't give herself permission to think. Instead, she zoned out to a popular romantic fantasy audiobook she downloaded at the airport. It'd been forever since she listened to anything but true crime podcasts, so it was refreshing to lose herself in a more uplifting story. She didn't even notice they were landing until a flight attendant tapped her on the shoulder to bring her seat upright.

Jules sped through the airport, pulling her carry-on behind her, surprised to see Winnie already parked on the arrivals curb, waving a hand out the open window.

As soon as Jules climbed into the tiny car, she pounced.

"I've been dying in anticipation. Spill, lady," she said, pulling off the curb, barely missing a utility van driving past.

"Focus, Winnie, I'd like to make it back in one piece."

"Hush, hush. *You* asked *me* to pick you up, didn't you?"

Jules laughed. "Yes, I suppose that's my fault. Thank you, though." She decided to just let it out. "So, I quit my job and have no idea what I'm going to do."

Winnie swung her head around, mouth wide open in a rare moment of speechlessness.

"Winnie!" Jules shouted. "Watch the road!"

"Jules!" Now, a huge smile plastered Winnie's face. "I'm so proud of you! I could tell that job was sucking your soul."

"Really? I didn't even realize it myself until yesterday when I found out my boss was sleeping with the secretary."

Winnie shot Jules another dumbfounded look, mouth hanging open.

"Yeah, I genuinely had no clue. I feel like an idiot."

"Is this the same boss who wants you to come work for her?"

"'Tis the same one, indeed. But obviously, I'm not doing that."

"I don't blame you," Winnie said before giving Jules some side eye and adding, "So, does this mean you're moving back to Riverbend? That we get to keep you?"

Jules had given little thought to that possibility in the few brief hours since she'd upended her life. Could she move back here for good? Or at least until she figured out what she was going to do? Maybe. It wasn't out of the question.

"I don't know. I still have my apartment in D.C., but I guess other than that, I wouldn't be leaving much behind. We'll just have to see how things go," she said, not ready to commit to anything.

"Well, either way, I say we celebrate! We should throw a party at my place and invite Miles."

"No," replied Jules. "I mean, let's celebrate, yes. But no to inviting Miles. I have too much to sort out without overcomplicating things." Jules desperately wanted to see Miles, but she knew it wasn't a good idea. After how she left and the feelings that were beginning to resurface, it was the last thing she needed.

"Ok. No Miles, just us. And maybe a few neighbors and other teachers? Only the cool ones, I promise," she said, plans already forming in her head. Jules knew Winnie was dying to know more about the Miles situation, but she also knew when to let it go. Jules would tell her more when she was ready.

Sitting back, she relaxed into the seat and agreed to go along with whatever Winnie planned, determined to lean into her newfound era of spontaneity. Although, she wasn't looking forward to having the same conversation with her grandma when she got home. She'd have to tell her she quit her job, and she didn't know how her grandma would react to the news. Would she be disappointed or impressed with Jules' bravery?

Once they crossed the county line to Riverbend, the reality of her situation started to creep in, forming stormy clouds of doubt in her mind. Would Grandma Rosa think she screwed up and was now crawling back home just like her mom had done so many times before? Would she understand, or would she tell her to go back to D.C. and beg for her job back? Jules wished for the serene calm she'd felt earlier to come back.

Trying to buy herself a few more minutes, she snuck in the front door with her luggage, hoping to get settled back in before breaking the news.

As soon as she stepped into the living room, a loud, "Jules!" rang from the kitchen.

Shit, she muttered under her breath.

Chapter 13

"Welcome home!" Grandma Rosa shouted.

Jules dropped her bags at the bottom of the stairs and made her way to the kitchen. No hiding now. She'd have to own what she'd done to the one person she cared the most. Turning into the kitchen, she let out the breath she'd been holding. The space was warm and cozy. It smelled of delicious bread baking in the oven and fresh coffee her grandma must have just put on. The well-loved table spilled over with newspapers, as usual. For a brief second, it felt like she had stepped back in time to her childhood, where nothing could hurt her and she didn't have to make big, life-altering decisions.

Looking up from her crossword puzzle, Grandma Rosa opened her arms for a hug and Jules relaxed. This was her grandma after all, the woman who raised her and was perpetually proud. Even if she didn't say it that often. Which was exactly the reason Jules didn't want to let her down. Although Rosa never understood what Jules did in D.C., she was the first to tell someone that her granddaughter worked a big fancy job in our Capital city. Nerves still pulsed through her veins, and she felt lightheaded as she took a seat.

"So how was the trip? Get everything done that you needed to?" Grandma Rosa asked.

"The hearing went well. No issues there." Jules avoided eye contact, but her grandma wouldn't let it go that easy, Jules knew.

Setting her crossword puzzle aside, Rosa stretched her hand across the table to Jules.

"Go on…"

"Umm," Jules fumbled, trying to find the right words. "Other things didn't go exactly as planned. I found out my boss is sleeping with the secretary, I saw Luke, and I quit my job," she said, ticking them off on her fingers.

After a beat, she faced her grandma, trying to hold her head high.

"But I'm good. It was the right thing to do. Now I have closure."

For a second, Rosa said nothing, just held Jules' gaze as if assessing whether or not to believe her.

"Wonderful. That's that, then. You can get on with the rest of your life now," she said in a serious tone, nodding her head.

"That's it? You're not going to tell me I made a mistake? That I'm throwing away my career?"

"No, I will not say that because it's not true. I'm proud of you. You made the right decision for what you need now. Rarely are the right decisions the easy ones."

Jules hung her head, looking into her lap. She didn't know what to say.

"You're not your mother, Jules. I know you've always feared being like her, but you're not. You will figure this out. It will be good. *You* will be good," she said as she squeezed Jules' hand. "I'm here for you, whatever you need."

"You always are. Thank you," Jules replied, smiling now. "And I hope you mean it because you might be stuck with me a little longer than we thought."

"I'd love that more than anything."

"Now tell me what's baking in the oven?"

And just like that, the conversation was over. The only thing Jules had to worry about now was the rest of her life, like her grandma had said.

Later that night, Val came over for dinner and card games. Jules helped her grandma make chicken piccata to serve with the fresh focaccia she had baked. Although she was hanging out with two women in their eighties, Jules enjoyed the night immensely. These women were a tad vulgar and loved to give each other a hard time, all out of love, though.

Within the first half an hour of Val's visit, Jules' stomach ached from all the laughing. At one point or another throughout the visit, Jules heard multiple insults hurled from one another like, "Stop being such a blunderbuss, you ole clack-box," and "Get out of my way, Miss Fussbudget." Jules had no idea what they meant, but she loved how their insults were both quaint and offensive at the same time.

Later, they made their way to the living room to play gin rummy around the old metal folding table Rosa always had in the corner for nights like these. Both Val and Rosa were notorious cheats, but they enjoyed playing whenever they could.

After a few rounds, Val blurted out, "Now tell me about that boy who helped you drop off the food for the ladies at The Landing the other night."

Jules should have known this question would come up. She'd been trying not to think about him since she'd gotten back to Riverbend. His silence had disappointed part of her, but she didn't blame him after she'd just walked out on him the other day. It was for the best, anyway.

"There's nothing to tell, really. He's an old friend."

"Oh, honey, we all know the history. Are you two back together?" Val asked, not skirting around the bush.

"No, we're not. I have too much to figure out without the complication of a relationship right now. Plus, there's a reason we didn't work out the first time," Jules answered, sure of herself.

"That's too bad, he's a looker."

Jules laughed, if she only knew.

"But, curious, what do you have to figure out?"

Jules filled Val in on her recent decisions, while Rosa nodded, chiming in about how strong and independent Jules has always been. It felt good to share without fear of judgment. Jules would have to learn to own this decision, and tonight was helping.

Out of nowhere, Val slapped her cards down on the table, accidentally showing her hand.

"I have an idea!" she shouted. "Since you'll have more free time and I assume you'll be around for a little longer, why don't you cook for the ladies a few nights a week at The Landing? We'll pay you, of course! And you can use the big commercial kitchen and all!"

"That's a wonderful suggestion," Grandma Rosa said in shared excitement.

Jules thought about it and shrugged her shoulders. Why not? It's not like her grandma needed her here every night. She was doing just fine on her own. Plus, it would be nice to keep cooking and stretching her skills. It was the only thing that gave her a sense of accomplishment lately. She could use more of that in her life right now. It would give her an opportunity to make more of her grandma's recipes with access to a fully stocked and large kitchen at her disposal.

"Ok, sure. When do I start?" she asked.

"How about tomorrow?"

"How about Monday?" Jules replied. Tomorrow, Jules would be at the celebration 'party' Winnie was planning, and she didn't want to make her reschedule.

"Done," said Val before they got back to playing their card game.

Although Jules didn't win a single hand all night, she loved seeing her grandma having fun. It had been years since she'd heard Rosa laugh with her whole body. It was the way her grandpa used to make her laugh with his silly, and often terrible, jokes, and tonight she heard it several times.

Even with the looming unknown hanging over her head, Jules knew she had a strong support system that wouldn't let her fail. She vowed to never let them down, either. A warm sensation spread through her chest as she recounted the evening later that night, lying in bed, just before dozing off. The peace didn't last; recollections of Miles singing to her plagued her dreams all night long.

***

Before the party on Sunday night, Jules agreed to join Winnie at the dress rehearsal of *Our Town* at the high school. It would be the first time the students rehearsed the play start to finish, costumes and all. When Winnie called Jules to ask for her help, she reeked of nervous energy. To be fair, it was the first time she'd directed a school play, and she didn't exactly know what she was doing. Not that Jules had any more experience either, but she was happy to be there for her in any way she could. While Jules got ready, throwing on a pair of jeans and a flowy top she could wear to the party later, she received a text message from Miles.

Attached to the message was a picture of the eighth hole on Riverbend's only golf course, Old Elm Club. Of course, she knew the place. It was the same golf course Miles had worked at the summer of their junior year, along with several other odd jobs. And hole eight had a special history with them.

Jules remembered the first time they snuck onto it. It was a warm, dewy summer night with not a single cloud overhead. He'd picked her up at her grandparents' just before sunset and drove the backroads to the staff entrance off the main road.

He parked behind the large dumpsters at the edge of the lot and led her to the back door of the white shiplap club house, where he took out the set of keys the owners gave him to lock up at night and used them to open the door, tilting his head to her with a conspiratorial smile. She remembered smacking his shoulder, whispering that they could get caught. He just waved her off and told her they had to live a little.

After they'd plundered the kitchen for leftover sandwich bread, cheese, and some pasta, they hiked through the course to hole eight, where Miles had left a blanket in the woods earlier that day. He'd planned it all out.

Hole eight was the most difficult and private hole on the entire course. Surrounded by walls of tall pine trees on three sides, the hole opened to a shallow pond just below the hill it sat on. It was the perfect spot for a picnic dinner beneath the stars without anyone spotting them. And so that's what they did, as often as they could the summer before their senior year. It was where they lost their virginities together on the checkered blanket Miles kept in the back of the car he borrowed from his cousin. It became their spot, one of the only places they could be alone together.

Jules stared at the phone screen for a minute, heart hammering in her chest. She owed Miles an explanation, she knew that. And his text meant he was testing the waters, likely wondering if their time together had come to an end, again.

Jules didn't know how to respond. They weren't together now, but they weren't just "friends" either. If she was going to give herself the time and space to figure out what she wanted out of life next, it meant being honest not only with herself, but with the people in her life, which now included Miles. She typed out a brief text and hit send.

> *Hey. It went well, thanks. Can you meet me at the high school at 3 p.m.? There's something I want to talk to you about. Thanks.*

It sounded ominous, but she did not want to have this conversation via text. They were adults now. It should be done face-to-face. Plus, he needed to know she meant it when she told him she wanted to be friends, even if he couldn't or wouldn't do that.

Miles responded with a thumbs-up.

Pulling into the parking lot just before three o'clock, she spotted Miles' convertible already parked in the staff section with his golf clubs still poking out of the backseat, waiting. He was wearing a light blue polo shirt, his skin a tanned gold that made his green eyes stand out even more in the bright sun of midday. Her heart fluttered at the sight as she slid into the spot next to him and climbed out and into his passenger seat. She was more nervous than she expected.

"Hey. How was your round of golf?" she asked as casually as she could.

"Fine. It was a good day for it." Then he turned toward her and asked, "What did you want to talk about?"

Ok, so no easing into it, Jules thought to herself. It's better this way.

"Well, I know I haven't told you much about my personal life and that's because it's kind of been up in the air," she said, not intending to be so vague. "But after my trip back to D.C., I realized I...I don't know..." She paused, trying to find the right words. "I don't know what I want."

Miles said nothing, just held her gaze. He was going to let her say whatever she needed to.

"While I was back in D.C., I quit my job, and I don't know what comes next. But I need to figure it out. Everything feels so...uncertain right now."

She looked at her hands clasped in her lap and continued, "Seeing you again was unexpected and wonderful, but I think it's best if we keep things simple for now, just friends. I can't handle much more, which is why I left in a rush the other day." Her voice was barely a whisper.

Miles still didn't respond, as if processing her words.

"I'll understand if that's not what you want, but it would mean a lot to me if we could try. You mean a lot to me. I don't want to lose you, again," she said, words running together.

She hated how desperate she sounded, but she couldn't imagine going back to the way it was before, when they didn't know each other anymore. And now, sharing the same space, it was hard to remain resolute in her decision. More than anything, she wanted to lean over the center console and kiss him hard, run her fingers through his tousled hair. She wanted his soft, warm lips to close around hers as he caressed the side of her face like he always did.

His silence punctuated the air between them. Jules held her breath, waiting for his response.

"You mean a lot to me, too. You always have, Jules. Every day since prom, I have regretted letting you go and not fighting harder for us. But at the time, I thought it was for the best, though it's haunted me. I've missed having you in my life. So, if friendship is all you can offer, I can try." Miles paused. "Although, I have plenty of those already," he added with a smirk, dissolving the taut tension, although Jules could see the disappointment in the way he kept his body rigid.

"Could you take on one more, for me?" she asked, lacing her fingers together in front of her, relaxing her shoulders. She hoped they could find a way to stay connected.

"Of course."

"Thank you. But, how did you know I was back in town?"

"Well, obviously not from you," he said, a slight edge in his voice before adding a smirk. "Greg, one of the science teachers here, texted me last night asking if I was going to the party Winnie was throwing for one of her friends, 'Jules'. Although, I had no idea what he was talking about."

"Ahh, sorry about that. That's my fault. I wanted to talk to you first," she said, stretching the truth. "But you're welcome to come tonight! It's just an excuse for Winnie to throw a party."

Jules was embarrassed she asked Winnie not to invite him. Of course, he'd hear about it.

"Thanks, I'll think about it."

That's all Jules could ask him to do.

After their rendezvous in the school parking lot, Jules felt conflicted at best. She was glad he took the conversation well. But in truth, part of her wanted him to talk her out of it. Convince her they'd be good together and should give it a proper go this time. But Miles was respectful. Always had been, and that wouldn't change now.

The dress rehearsal was set to start at three thirty, so she hurried inside to find a stressed and frantic Winnie hurling demands at the students backstage as they got into their costumes and took their places.

"Hey, Win," Jules said, placing a tentative hand on her shoulder from behind, causing Winnie to whip around, almost losing her balance.

"Oh, thank God you're here," she said, hand over heart. "Talk me down, Jules. I don't know what's wrong with me."

Jules engulfed Winnie in a long hug before giving her a quick motivational talk.

"It's just pre-show jitters, that's all. And remember this is just the dress rehearsal. There's four more days to fine tune anything that needs it before opening night. You got this."

"Right. From now on, I'm a beacon of calm. I will be the lighthouse in the storm. Calm as an angel in the dragon's den," she said, hands lifted out to her sides, head back, with closed eyes.

"Yeah...be those." Jules chuckled. She loved her best friend, weird metaphors and all.

Within thirty seconds, Winnie was back to her high-pitched screeching, trying to locate the male lead, who was in the bathroom nursing a bad hangover from the cast party the night before. Winnie and Jules found him hunched over the toilet.

"I'm going to pretend that I don't know the real reason you're puking your guts out right now, and in exchange for that, you're going to get up and get on stage in no less than two minutes," Winnie said to him, kneeling down to be eye-level.

Making their way to the theater, Jules whispered, "Damn, Winnie, that was straight up mafia style."

"Kids these days are savage. They can smell weakness from a mile away."

"Whatever you say. You're the Don."

"They'd do good not to forget it, too," she said in a fake Italian accent, causing them to burst out laughing. Both knew

Winnie was the farthest from a 'Don' personality as one could get.

Overall, the rehearsal wasn't terrible. It wasn't good, either, but it could be fixed. The worst part was the drunk male lead who couldn't find his mark to save his life. Other than that, the cast only needed to memorize their lines, and they'd have a show.

On their way out to the parking lot afterwards, Winnie wondered aloud if she should call up the lead's understudy for Friday night's show, but Jules convinced her to give him one more chance. Didn't she remember the shenanigans they got up to in high school? Maybe he'd kick it into high gear for the next rehearsal.

"We'll see," said Winnie, already tired. "Meet you there?"

"Sure thing, boss," Jules shot back before sliding into Rosa's Subaru.

She hoped an evening of socialization would help Winnie relax. All afternoon her friend became more tightly wrung, as if she were a jack-in-the-box waiting to explode. It was very unlike Winnie. Something was off.

Chapter 14

Jules was amazed by how much effort Winnie and Emily had put into the party. It was only supposed to be an intimate get-together, a reason to see friends, but throughout the house hung streamers and banners that read, 'Welcome Back' and 'The Jule is Back in Town'. She didn't know what to say and wondered why they'd go through this much trouble just because she was back for a few weeks. Didn't they realize it wasn't a permanent thing?

Jules groaned at the thought of having to correct everyone tonight when they asked her about it.

Sensing her apprehension, Emily looped her arm through Jules' and steered her into the kitchen where she had been arranging charcuterie boards full of deli meats, sliced cheeses, grapes, nuts, and olives. Bottles of white wine were chilling in metal buckets of ice on the kitchen island next to bottles of red and empty wine glasses ready to be filled.

"I know it's a lot," said Emily in a hushed voice. Winnie had gone to change her clothes before people arrived, so it was just the two of them. "But Winnie needed a distraction. She's been out of her mind with worry about the play and other things," she said, waving her hand in the air. "I hope you don't mind all the fuss."

Jules understood. Throwing herself into things helped Winnie during stressful times. It was her coping mechanism.

"I don't mind. I'm flattered but also a bit worried people will think I'm moving back for good," Jules said, helping Emily slice the last of the two blocks of Gouda. "I'm not sure what I'm doing, and I don't know how to explain it to people yet."

Emily cocked her head in thought. "Well, fuck 'em. Just say you're working on a confidential project. It's technically not a lie. You are working on *you*. You don't owe anyone the details, especially not these people."

Jules knew Emily was right. She didn't owe anyone anything right now, besides her grandmother. At that moment, she decided she was going to enjoy the night and not worry too much about what people she didn't know anymore thought about her.

She gave Emily a tight side hug at the counter and said, "Thank you. I think that's exactly what I'll do."

The night progressed, with people showing up at six on the dot, toting in more bottles of wine to add to the kitchen collection. A few men held what looked like expensive whiskey bottles, but Jules knew nothing about brown liquor, only that she didn't have a taste for it. Jules kept a watchful eye on the front door for the first hour, expecting, hoping, for Miles to walk in, but he never did. *It's for the best*, she thought to herself after a while.

What she saw, however, was Winnie following Emily around like a nervous child, asking every few minutes if she felt alright, wanted to sit, or needed water. She had insisted on bringing Emily a plate of food and then making a show of rubbing her shoulders. At one point, Jules made up a reason she needed Winnie's help in the kitchen, just to give Emily a few minutes of space, which was returned with a wordless 'thank you' from Emily.

To Jules' surprise, she knew almost everyone at the party, except for a few spouses who tagged along. It was amazing to her how many people who grew up in Riverbend stayed and made their lives here. And for the most part, they seemed happy. Many of them were teachers in the school district, but a few commuted to work in Chicago.

The conversations were easy going, and no one asked or even seemed to care much what she did for a living, which was a refreshing change. In D.C., it was one of the first questions asked when you met someone: *What do you do?* It was the way people sized each other up out there. *How important are you? Are you worth knowing or just a waste of time?* Not here. People were genuinely nice and talked about the local football team, their kids, or what they were growing in their gardens.

Even some friends she hadn't seen since high school were there. After making a first round through the party greeting guests, she tucked herself away in a cozy corner of the living room with two friends, reminiscing and catching up. She'd missed a lot in the past twelve years: Jill already had four kids!

Jules couldn't even imagine having one kid, let alone four. But her friend beamed with pride as she swiped through pictures of them on her phone. Her other friend, Veronica, played in the Chicago Philharmonic. Impressed, Jules asked her why she still lived in Riverbend rather than move to the city.

"My life is here. My family and friends. Right now, it works for me. But maybe in the future, I'll end up somewhere else. Who knows?" she said, shrugging her shoulders.

That made Jules' mind spin off in a new direction. Was anything ever truly permanent? Just because you might decide to do a thing now or even for a period of time, it doesn't mean you have to do it forever, right? She liked the idea of reinvention and trying on multiple versions of herself. It differed from how her Grandma Rosa approached life, and veered dangerously close to her mother's ideology, but the notion intrigued her. Could she change her way of thinking from black and white to a more flexible approach? Running into Veronica shifted Jules' thinking at the exact right time.

Later that night, after all the guests had left and Emily had gone to bed early, exhausted from the day, Winnie and Jules cleaned up. They were rinsing dishes in the sink when Jules asked Winnie if she was alright. It was as if someone had let the air out of an overfilled balloon; Winnie hung her head and slumped her shoulders forward over the sink, letting out a long, heavy sigh.

"I'm sorry," she said in a small voice as a sob leaked out.

Jules grabbed her friend, wrapping her arms around Winnie's shoulders. She hadn't seen her this worried since her mother's battle with breast cancer a few years ago.

"You can tell me anything, or we don't have to talk. I can just hold you if that's what you need," she said.

Winnie turned away, making her way to the pedestal table set in an alcove of windows near the back of their kitchen, as Jules followed.

"I'm just a bundle of anxiety lately," she started. "I know I'm on Emily's last nerve, but I can't help it."

"What's going on? Anything I can help with?" Jules asked.

"No, you're already helping by giving me a distraction and support for the play. But it's all just a lot right now. The play, the pregnancy, everything." Jules just nodded along, encouraging her friend to continue. "I'm so excited for the baby. But I'm also scared as shit."

"It must be so scary to know you'll have to take care of a small human soon," Jules agreed.

"It's not just that, which yes, is terrifying on its own," she said looking up at Jules before taking a deep breath. "Last year, we lost a baby. Emily had a miscarriage around the fourteen-week mark, which is where she's at right now."

Jules felt punched in the gut. How could she not have known? It all made sense now.

"Oh, Win, I'm so sorry." Jules reached for her hand.

"It's alright. The doctor says the baby is healthy and growing, so we should focus on other things. But I just can't seem to do that. It's all I think about."

Jules heart ached for her friend, who did not know how close to home her news hit.

"Whatever you need, please know that I'm here for you and Emily. I love you guys so much."

"We love you, too. Who knows how bad I'd be if you weren't here."

Jules was glad she was home and could give Winnie support this time, but hearing about what happened made her feel guilty for being so self-centered. Jules had only focused on herself since the break-up with Luke, obsessing over her own life, and had missed that her friend was suffering a traumatic loss. She knew the ache of going through something like that alone.

"I promise I'll stick around for anything you need." And she meant it.

***

Her first shift cooking dinner at The Landing came sooner than expected. Jules spent most of Monday morning shopping for the ingredients she'd need to make a large batch of mozzarella and basil stuffed chicken that she planned to serve with fresh bread and a light, crispy Italian salad. The menu had popped into her head last night just as she was drifting off, causing her to click on her table light and jot down a shopping list and schedule for the next day. She got little sleep.

Filling her cart with food and seasonings at John's Shoppe, her excitement grew alongside her nerves. She was looking forward to cooking in a large commercial-grade kitchen for the first time, but she worried she wouldn't know how to use everything, so she rushed to give herself extra time.

Arriving two hours before she needed to, she was surprised to find Grandma Rosa waiting for her as she hauled the bags of groceries into the large, all stainless-steel kitchen.

"What are you doing here?" Jules exclaimed.

"I thought you could use some help on your first day. It's been a while, but I used to know my way around a kitchen like this," she said, gazing at the space, which appeared to be brand new. "I had a feeling you'd come early."

"Why does it look like no one has ever cooked in here?"

Just then, Val rounded the corner.

"That's because this is the special 'catering' kitchen they put in for what they thought would be special meals for holidays and such. They built it for outside caterers, but that never happened," Val explained. "Until you!"

Jules' belly flipped with anticipation to get her hands on the equipment. But first, she needed to do a thorough inventory of the place to find out what she was working with.

"I'll let you ladies get to it," Val said before slipping back out.

For the next few hours, Jules and Rosa worked side by side, taking occasional breaks to rest. The time flew by as her grandma showed her how to prep everything she'd need before cooking and later how to cook the food so it would go out on time and be warm. It was hard work.

By the end of service, both were exhausted, yet proud of the meal they'd put together. They'd heard some 'oohs' and 'ahhs' as the food went out to the dining room and later received many compliments from the diners. It was a successful first night and the first time she hadn't thought about her future or Miles on a constant loop since arriving back in Riverbend.

After helping the wait staff give the kitchen a good scrub, they headed home late in the evening. The night sky darkened with clouds, and a slight autumn chill caused Jules' skin to prickle with goosebumps.

Upon arriving back at her grandma's, Jules headed straight to the kitchen to make two cups of warm chamomile tea.

As Jules warmed the kettle on the stove, her grandma sat, slipping her shoes off to rub her feet. "So have you seen Miles at all?" she asked.

"Umm, yes. Yesterday for a few minutes."

"I take it you're cooling things off for a bit?"

"It's the right thing to do," Jules responded, biting the inside of her cheek as she filled the two mugs and set them on the table.

Her grandmother let out a moan of pleasure as she sipped her tea, humming a song Jules didn't recognize. She was either too tired to respond or was letting Jules have space when it came to Miles.

After a few moments of silence, she asked, "How's your mother?" It was the first time Grandma Rosa had mentioned Barb in the last few weeks.

"She seems good. Better than I've seen her in a long time," responded Jules. "She's going to school to be a vet tech, you know."

Grandma Rosa's eyes widened in surprise.

"Well, that's nice, I suppose. Where is she living now?"

"She's in Naperville. Living by herself. Well, I guess with a cat, too."

"Oh. I don't think she's ever lived alone."

Knowing this could be an opportunity to help heal things between her mother and her grandma, Jules treaded lightly. "She seems happy and determined to finish her studies while working. I'm cautiously optimistic."

"Hmm. We'll see," Grandma Rosa said, rising from her chair. "I'm going to call it a night and get some shut-eye. You should, too."

"I'm right behind you. Just need to rinse the cups," Jules said. "Thanks for your help tonight. It meant a lot to me you were there."

"You would have been just fine on your own, but I wanted you to know that you always have support," she said before disappearing around the corner to climb the stairs for bed.

Sitting alone in her grandma's kitchen, Jules felt the familiar blanket of comfort that she knew so well growing up. This was the place she always went when she needed advice, comfort food, or just to be with someone who loved and cared about her. Although it wasn't much more than a modest kitchen, it was everything to her. She may not know what the future looked like, but she was sure this kitchen would always feel like home.

That evening, sleep washed over her like a steady wave. Both her mind and body were empty, and she fell into a deep slumber that caused her to wake with start when she glanced at her alarm clock that read ten in the morning. She hadn't slept that late since college. But it didn't matter since she had no plans for the day. Her next shift at The Landing wasn't until the following evening, so she did the thing she'd been putting off: catching up on emails. Surely, they'd contain official instructions for ending her employment at the Treasury Department. She'd written her resignation letter last week before her flight home but hadn't paid it any attention since.

At the top of her inbox sat a message from the Human Resources department outlining next steps and other details about her benefits. Jules groaned, deciding to deal with it later.

Scrolling down, a message from a name she didn't recognize caught her eye. It was a journalist from the *Washington Post*, asking her to call him to chat about her employment. She hesitated. If they wanted her to give them inside information about the secretary, she wouldn't do it. It wasn't her story to tell, and Jules didn't want to be the reason his wife found out about his affair, if she wasn't already aware. But the journalist had been vague enough to pique her curiosity. What could he want with her? Her head swam with possibilities as she reached for her phone.

Benjamin McAllister picked up on the second ring with a proper eastern seaboard accent in tow.

"Hi, this is Jules Cuccia. You emailed me yesterday."

"Hi, Miss Cuccia. Thanks for taking the time to phone," he responded as they dispensed of the common pleasantries.

"I wanted to talk to you about your recent resignation from the U.S. Treasury Department. You were Secretary Monahan's Chief Speechwriter, correct?" he asked.

Jules responded with a suspicious, "Yes."

"And before that, you wrote for several members of Congress, correct?"

Another curt, "Yes," from Jules. "What is this about, Mr. McAllister?" she added. She wanted him to get to the point already.

"Well, I would love to know why you resigned from your latest role but also wanted to inform you we have an opening on our staff here at *WaPo*. Given your background, I think you might be a good fit for it."

Jules didn't quite understand. Was he offering her a job? And was it in exchange for a scoop? She couldn't tell.

Picking up on the discomfort coming from her silence, he added, "I'm only interested in your resignation as it pertains to your current employment status. Are you available for and interested in other professional opportunities?"

Interesting, Jules thought. Was she open to other opportunities? She hadn't considered that people would seek her out this fast.

"Possibly. But may I ask how you found out about my resignation? I haven't told many people yet."

"It was in a news bulletin the Department sends to the Associated Press each Monday."

That made sense. Becca was trying to get ahead of things, although she'd never considered that her resignation would constitute news.

"Got it. Tell me more about the open role," said Jules.

Benjamin explained the role was new, and they were looking for a professional writer, not a journalist, to pen a weekly column about Federal and Congressional staff in the D.C. area. The vision would be to give a voice to government workers and the issues that mattered most to them, highlighting what their day-to-day looked like. Apparently, she was an ideal candidate because she was an experienced writer, had worked in government, and of course already lived in the district.

It sounded intriguing, but she wasn't sure if jumping into another job right away was wise. Not to mention, it was a role that would ensure she lived and breathed all that was D.C. But it was *WaPo*, after all.

"Could you send me the job description and give me a day or two to think it over?" she asked.

"Of course. If you are interested, the next step would be a chat with our editor, who is eager to meet you," Benjamin informed her.

The editor of the *Washington Post* wanted to meet *her*? It felt surreal. She needed time to think things through, so Jules told him she'd follow up with him before Thursday.

To clear her head and get her blood flowing again after a night of dead-to-the-world sleep, Jules threw on her tennis shoes and hopped out the front door for a quick run. She usually avoided running as exercise, but she needed to move and feel the blood rush through her veins. Plus, she didn't have access to a fancy gym here like the one in her apartment building in D.C. This would have to do.

Deciding to head towards Main Street, she eased into a slow pace that might leave her able to reach downtown and back. Overhead, the sun beamed through large white fluffy clouds that gave her cover every few minutes, making the temperature mild and pleasant.

As she ran by the '50s and '60s rambler-style houses in her grandma's neighborhood, she could smell the fresh scent of cut grass. The street was quiet except for the chirp of birds in the trees, but no one was outside, thankfully. Jules didn't feel like talking. She'd neglected to put on any makeup or even brush her hair.

As she ran, the anxiety that pressed against her throat after her conversation with Benjamin eased, replaced by deepening breaths growing in rhythm with her steady steps. She passed the downtown shops, including the new coffee shop, John's, and Nicholson's hardware, deciding to turn around at the end of the business district to grab coffee on her way back.

The young maple trees lining main street were showing signs of fall as their leaves had turned a bright yellow at the tips. In just a few short weeks, the trees would be an array of yellows, vibrant reds, and deep purples before littering the ground, giving the town the unmistakable aroma of autumn that Jules knew so well. She realized she wanted to see the change. Fall was never quite the same anywhere else.

Looping around the ornate early nineteenth-century bank at the end of Main Street, Jules made her way back to the coffee shop, entering under the hand-painted sign reading "Drips" over the red and white striped awning. A few customers queued at the register, but the line moved quickly.

Iced vanilla latte in hand, Jules took a few minutes to sip while reading the assortment of fliers hanging from the community bulletin board in the back of the cozy shop. One flier promoted a sketch comedy show for that Saturday in Wicker Park, a part of Chicago she was familiar with.

Winnie loved comedy shows. They used to watch Saturday Night Live together every weekend growing up and took trips into Chicago to see Second City shows once they were old enough.

An idea formed; maybe she and Winnie could go into the city Saturday to see the show? They could make a whole day of it.

"That's perfect," Jules said to herself, snapping a picture of the flier.

Friday night was the one and only night *Our Town* would run, so it could also be a celebration of sorts. Not to mention, it would give Emily almost a full day to herself. Jules called Winnie to lay out her plan. She was in.

Taking her time to walk back to her grandma's, Jules noticed all the renovated houses she passed. The area looked the same as how she remembered it from years ago, only now it felt like someone had given it a good scrub and fresh coat of paint, leaving it glistening and new. Riverbend looked more like a historic suburb now, rather than the small farming town where she grew up. The improvements left her feeling proud but also nostalgic for the past. Everything seemed like it was changing, even the place that had been the one constant in her life.

Before turning back onto her street, her phone chirped with a text. It was Miles.

Chapter 15

At the sight of his name on her phone, Jules' body went warm. A part of her desperately wanted to see him but wasn't sure if it was a good idea.

Ultimately, desire outweighed her better judgement and she convinced herself it would be fine. For one, she had no plans and wasn't cooking for the ladies at The Landing. And two, she wanted to see how Roxy and Jax were doing. She had to be close to popping by now!

She rewrote her text a few times before sending it, not wanting to come off too eager.

Jules cursed the butterflies in her stomach as she walked through the front door of her grandma's house. Her body was betraying her mind, and she needed to get a hold on that fast. Friends. That's all she could offer right now.

The rest of the day was a blur as a slew of repairmen that she'd hired came to fix the various things around the house that needed tending. Between greeting them and playing defense from her grandmother's incessant hovering and snide comments, she lost track of time before noticing the microwave clock read six p.m. She wanted to be there when Miles' set started.

Hurrying upstairs to change, she gathered her hair in a sleek ponytail. The dark auburn color was dulling, most likely because she'd missed her regular six-week touch-up at the beginning of the month. Maybe she would let it keep growing out to her natural color. She wondered if she had any greys yet as she made her way out the door. It would have to do for now.

The gastropub was quiet when she arrived, with only a handful of people scattered around the bar, and Miles was already on stage, preparing his sound equipment. As she slid into an empty bar stool, he gave her a tight smile, which she thought was odd. Maybe he was in a hurry and wanted to start on time.

Her stomach growled, so she ordered some food and a drink, a welcome distraction. A few moments later, Jax came over to say hello.

"Where's Roxy?" Jules asked as he wiped off the bar top with a wet rag.

"She's at home, resting. She might come later, but her back has been killing her."

"Everything ok with her and the baby?"

"Oh, yeah. Everything is fine. She's just ready to not be pregnant anymore," he said with a hoarse laugh. "How come I haven't seen you here in a while? What's going on with you and our guy over there?"

Jules twirled the bottom of the water glass in her hand on the counter.

"Well—" she started.

"Ahh, I see. Trouble in paradise," he interrupted.

"Not exactly. We agreed to be friends while I figure some stuff out," she continued.

"That explains why he's been so sulky. Could barely get more than two words out of him this past week."

Jules' cheeks reddened. It made her uncomfortable that Jax knew this much about their relationship. He probably thought she was an awful person, her coming back into town and leading Miles on. But no one knew their full history, or why they didn't work the first time around. Jules and Miles even had secrets from each other.

Sensing the discomfort, he asked if she was planning to stay in town for a while or if she was going back to D.C. soon.

"I might stay around for a little longer. It depends on a few things," she said. Jules hadn't quite figured out what those few things were, but she was working on it.

For the next hour, she ate her gourmet fish and chips, which looked like they belonged on the cover of a food magazine, and listened to Miles sing. His voice seemed far away, almost underwater and she wondered if it had anything to do with her being there. He avoided looking her way and when he did, he averted his eyes down to his guitar. It didn't take her long to feel like an outsider again, like she wasn't welcome here.

Luckily, she didn't have too long to think about it before Roxy walked in and plopped down in the chair next to her. Jules couldn't believe she was even walking at this point. Her shirt, a dark green button-down that probably belonged to Jax's, stretched over her round belly that had almost doubled in size since the last time she saw her.

"Oh, my word. How are you feeling?" Jules asked, turning away from the stage.

"Oh, you know. Like a school bus," Roxy said, waving at her stomach. "I can't believe there's only one in there. I wouldn't be surprised if we came home with triplets. Just crossing my fingers I make it through next week."

"Next week?" Jules asked, confused.

"The Bear Ball."

"That's right. Sorry, I completely forgot it was coming up. Is the planning going well?"

Roxy told her she had the menu all planned out but was worried about the prep work. Her kitchen staff was flaky at best, and she needed all the help she could get in her current state.

"I have some extra time on my hands and would love to help," Jules offered.

"If you'd be willing, I'd appreciate it so much. I've heard you're a skilled cook from a few people at The Landing." Roxy's face looked pleading and relieved at the same time.

Jules told her she'd be glad to help and to email her the details. She'd be there. For someone without an actual job, she sure was keeping busy. However, she worried how Miles would feel about her volunteering. These were his friends, after all.

Two songs and a glass of wine later, Miles finished his set and packed up. Jules knew it would be her only chance to chat with him that night, so she made her way over to the stage.

"You sounded great," she said, which wasn't a lie. He did sound good, just different.

"Not my best performance, but it'll have to do," he responded as he continued to put his gear away, not bothering to make eye contact. There was a long stretch of uncomfortable silence before he added, "But thanks for coming."

Well, this was more awkward than she'd feared. Taking a deep breath and trying not to fidget like she always did when she was unsure of herself, Jules asked, "Are you upset with me?"

The question seemed to hang in the air between them for a few seconds before he turned to face her, letting out a long sigh.

"No, not exactly. It probably wasn't the best idea for you to be here tonight, though," he admitted, which flared up a lick of anger in Jules.

Without thinking, she shot back, "*You* invited *me*, remember?"

Holding his hands up defensively, he said, "I know…I know I did. And I thought I wanted you here. I always want you. That's the problem." Miles' head slumped down, shoulders rounding, heavy with an invisible weight.

Softening now at his honesty, Jules told him she understood. She felt the same way, which was part of the issue.

"But, friendship is all I can offer right now. Anything more and we're likely to hurt each other, again. I wish it were different, but it just isn't."

"That's just it. I don't know if I *know* how to be just your friend. We've always been more," he responded, starting directly at her now.

A pit in Jules' stomach grew. She didn't know how to be just his friend, either. Hell, just standing here, watching him put his guitar away in his tight light-washed blue jeans and signature black V-neck had her mind going to many unfriend-like places.

"Maybe it's best if we just give each other some space for a while to figure it out," he suggested, running his hand over his face.

She wanted to sink even farther into the floor. His words gutted her. And even though she knew he was right, it brought her right back to the summer after graduation, feeling alone and unwanted.

"Yeah. If that's what you think," she whispered. "I can give you space."

"Sorry, Jules. It's just a lot to process and I need to do it my own way." He turned away from her to pick up his guitar case and slung it over his shoulder.

She understood. This was her fault, after all. She should never have started anything with him she wasn't ready for. It could never just be easy and casual with Miles; she was a fool to think it could.

"Got it," she said, nodding and heading toward the door. "Guess I'll see you around, then. Bye, Miles."

She heard him say a quiet, "Bye, Jules," just before she reached the door, wondering if Jax, Roxy and the handful of other customers in the place heard all of that. God, she hoped not.

She hurried as fast as she could to the car without running, but before she could even turn the ignition, her tears welled over. How was she here, again? Crying over the same guy who'd shattered her heart into a million tiny shards years ago? Sitting alone in her grandma's Subaru, she made a deal with herself. She would let herself cry until she got home, and that's it. After that, she'd only look forward.

As she lurched the car in drive, she remembered she'd forgotten to tell him about helping Roxy with the school benefit. *Maybe this town was too small for both of them*, she thought to herself.

Taking it as a sign, she texted Benjamin from the *Washington Post* when she returned home to set up a time to connect the next day. It was time to explore her options.

***

Wednesday meant another evening cooking at The Landing. This time, Jules would be on her own. Earlier that day, Grandma Rosa had not so subtly told her it was "sink or swim." Jules had a feeling her great-grandfather had given Rosa more than one lesson in the restaurant kitchen before leaving her to her own devices.

But if Jules was anything, she was a planner, so it didn't take long for her to come up with a detailed list of what she needed for that night's menu which she could cook in her sleep: an easy spaghetti pomodoro with a roasted zucchini and red pepper side. For dessert, pies from John's Shoppe would have to do. Baking was never her strong suit, anyway.

Jules rushed through her shopping list and made it to the retirement community with hours to spare. She had a call with Benjamin that afternoon, too.

After organizing the ingredients and necessary cooking tools, she prepped by chopping the tomatoes, zucchini, and red peppers until her hand felt as if it might fall off. Didn't most chefs have kitchen staff? Needing to prove to herself and her grandma she could do this, she pressed on, knowing she'd be sore tomorrow. Gone were her days of sitting at a computer typing away, although she didn't much mind. Cooking at this scale kept both her hands and mind busy for hours at a time, leaving little room to think about anything else.

By the time everything was chopped, trimmed, and simmering in a large pot, Jules had just a few minutes to gather her thoughts before ringing Benjamin at the agreed time. Surprised to find herself nervous, she dialed his number in the back corner of the quiet kitchen.

"Jules, so glad to hear from you, again!" he greeted her with a booming voice.

He seemed to genuinely like his job, which made Jules even more eager to tell him she was interested in working for *The Washington Post*, but she had some stipulations if they were to move forward.

For one, her time working for Secretary Monahan was off-limits, she would not talk about it. And second, she wanted to explore the option to work remotely with travel as needed.

"That all sounds reasonable. Why don't I set up a time for you to meet with our editor to discuss this more?"

Jules agreed.

Feeling powerful and in control of her future, Jules crushed the dinner service. Sure, it was a stressful few hours in the kitchen, but everything came together except for a few overcooked zucchinis that ended up in the trash.

Tired to the bone, she went home, wondering how professional chefs did that every night without their bodies giving out. Although exhausting, she was grateful for the opportunity to learn more about cooking, preparation, and self-reliance in a large kitchen. Not to mention, she didn't have time to think about Miles.

The editor of the *Washington Post* called Jules the next morning for the informal interview Benjamin had arranged. Julian Arnault was an accomplished journalist with over thirty years in the business. Jules had never met him, but anyone in D.C. who kept up with the news knew of him. He had more Pulitzer Prizes than she could count and was most recently an editor at the *New York Times* before taking on the role of *WaPo's* managing editor. To say she was nervous was an understatement. She couldn't keep her hands steady as she picked up the phone, standing to pace her childhood bedroom.

"Hello, is this Jules Cuccia?" Julian's voice boomed through the phone with an ambiguous accent. Mandatory pleasantries exchanged, Julian got right to business.

"So, I hear you may be interested in joining us as a regular columnist here at *WaPo*?"

"Yes, I spoke to Benjamin earlier this week and it sounds like an intriguing opportunity, but I'd love to hear more about your vision for the role," she countered, trying to sound calm and professional.

Julian gave her a quick overview, echoing what Benjamin had already shared, but ended by asking Jules about her thoughts on the role.

"I want to be transparent with you, Mr. Arnault," she started before he cut in, instructing her to call him Julian.

"Ok, Julian. I've always wanted to write for a major news outlet, as I did study journalism, but I'm not sure I'm the right person for this topic."

"Tell me more."

"I'm at a crossroads in my career and not sure what comes next. But I do know that it needs to challenge my creative side. I'm worried that this role will be similar in content to what I've been writing about as a speechwriter for the past ten years."

Jules was proud of herself for being so honest. A younger Jules would have leaped at this opportunity, yet here she was, telling Julian what *she* wanted first.

"I understand. When your name came across my desk, we thought it would be a perfect fit given your writing experience and your background. But I see why you'd want to explore other options," he said, which Jules took as a signal for ending the conversation.

However, after a brief pause, he continued, "I'll tell you what, why don't you think about what it is you *want* to write about? Then we can talk again in a few days. I see potential in you, and I'd like to explore how we can work together."

She'd expected this conversation to be short. A quick, "Thank you for considering the role, we have other candidates...," but it sounded like he wanted *her* to work there.

Jules told him she'd think about it, and they set up a time to reconnect early the following week. Never in her wildest dreams did she think Julian Arnault would offer her a job. Jules wasn't used to being sought after like this. Sure, she was relatively successful at what she did, and Becca had asked her to come work with her, too, but she didn't feel like that counted anymore.

For the most part, Jules had aggressively pursued every job she'd had, just like her accomplishments. The perseverance and grit that she'd developed at a young age, determined to have a future different from the other women in her family, had let her leave Illinois for college and move to D.C. days after graduation. She always knew what she wanted and worked hard to get it. But this time was different. Although Jules was out of her comfort zone, she could recognize an opportunity when it hit her in the face. She just needed to figure out how to make the most of it.

Now that Jules had concrete options ahead of her and not just the ambiguous black hole she'd been envisioning ever since she left D.C., time sped up. Thursday went by in a blink as she shopped for that evening's dinner ingredients and planned out the meal. The actual prep and cooking went even quicker, as her mind was elsewhere. All she could think about was her conversation with Julian. *What did she want to write about?*

Jules got so lost in her thoughts that she didn't even notice Val standing next to her at the stovetop that evening. Jules jumped when she felt a hand on her shoulder.

"Woah, I didn't mean to startle you, but I'm glad I did. Your chicken is burning," she said, pointing down to the sizzling pan in Jules' hand. She was right. Instead of searing the chicken, she'd charred one side to a black crisp.

"Shit," Jules sputtered. "It's ok, I'm almost done anyway. I'll fire up a few more," she said, rushing around the stainless-steel workspaces to grab the last of the chicken breasts from the large walk-in fridge.

"What's on your mind, Jules?" Val asked, watching her.

"Oh, just my future. No big deal," Jules said. She wasn't trying to come off rude. "Sorry, Val. I'm good, actually. Just a lot going on."

"Ok. Well, the ladies would like to know if you could join them for dinner tonight. You know, after you're done cooking? They'd love to thank you."

In a rush to finish on time now, Jules nodded yes, and Val disappeared back to the happy hour event that The Landing hosted every night. Jules wondered if they just wanted a new face to gossip about later. The ladies were lovely, but they fed on drama.

Even with a few burnt pieces of chicken, Grandma Rosa's recipe for *Petti Di Pollo al Burro*, Italian butter chicken, was a colossal hit. Jules served it family style in the dining room alongside enormous platters of cooked pasta and dressed greens. Eating, and now serving, family style meals were her favorite because they encouraged people to talk while they passed their plates. It was like an interactive version of dining. Even from the kitchen, she could hear the different conversations happening over the table. It filled her with joy and contentment. She had created this experience for them, and it made her happy to hear them so happy.

After the last main dish was served, Val came back to the kitchen a few glasses of wine heavier and dragged Jules to a table of women yelling to hear each other—they did all have hearing aids, after all.

The dining room was an ornate space, designed to look traditional yet upscale. Each of the tables sat up to six people and had lavish place settings that the wait staff set out before dinner. This wasn't their usual dining room, but it had gotten much more use for dinners now that Jules was cooking. Before that, it was only used as a meeting space for different groups and clubs. Val had commented earlier that week that the residents loved seeing it used for its original intention and Jules had to admit that it was an impressive room.

Following Val, she took the only other empty seat, as the room's attention turned towards Jules.

"Where did you learn to cook like this?" a woman with dyed black hair and very red lipstick demanded to know.

Before Jules could even answer, the lady sitting next to her yelled, "She's Rosa Cuccia's granddaughter, Bette. You know this!"

"Oh, leave her be, Flo. We all forget things," said another, patting Bette's hand. "Your food is wonderful, Jules. But what we all want to know is what is going on with that hunk of a man who helped you drop food off a few weeks ago. *Where* is he?" she asked, wiggling her eyebrows at her.

Oh lord.

"His name is Miles and we're just friends," she politely replied.

"That's a euphemism these days, ladies," another chimed in.

Luckily, Val came to her rescue, calming them down and returning the chatter back to Jules' cooking. All the women complimented Jules' food, some saying it had brought back memories of their mother's cooking from their childhoods in Chicago. It was amazing how many of them were Italian and had grown up close to Grandma Rosa. It really was a small world.

"Well, we are just grateful to have you here. We hope you don't go back to that big city full of blustering politicians anytime soon. Although, then maybe we'd see more of your grandma around here!" cooed Bette as she sloshed her wine around in the glass.

Just as Jules started to have a good time, her heart sank. She was mortified to think about the possibility of her grandmother living at The Landing if she went back to D.C. While these ladies seemed nice and lovely enough, she knew her grandma wouldn't want to live here. But what alternative would she have? Rosa couldn't take care of herself *and* the house anymore; it just wasn't feasible. The reality of it stung. While the *Washington Post* was a dream, her grandma was a priority.

Chapter 16

"They're animals, straight up savage beasts," Jules murmured to Winnie, watching in horror as about twenty high school kids descend upon the meal Jules brought to the school for their big night.

"At least they are using forks this time," Winnie responded, turning her back to the outrageous scene. Jules didn't want to know what that was in reference to, but she was glad they were enjoying the lasagna and bread she'd made.

"Thanks for bringing dinner. For some of them, it's the only home-cooked meal they've had all week."

To Jules' surprise, Winnie had been exceedingly calm since she'd arrived about an hour ago. *Our Town* was premiering tonight for one show only. The cast had turned things around since their first dress rehearsal. Winnie looked relaxed. She even seemed to enjoy the crazed energy buzzing through everyone backstage.

"I'm so proud of you, Win." Jules put her arm around Winnie's shoulders as they walked back to the dressing rooms.

"Don't jinx it! We still have to get through the show," she joked, but there was no hint of truth to it. Winnie was excited, and it was rubbing off on Jules, too. Jules had never been a big theater fan, but she couldn't wait to watch the kids do their thing, especially after all the hard work they'd put into it.

They poked their heads into the dressing room, making sure things were in place and people were getting ready, but a mini drama of its own was unfolding near the mirrored makeup stations. Several high school girls crowded around another who sobbed into her hands.

Winnie looked at Jules with wide eyes and a contrite smile before whispering, "Her boyfriend was caught with a cheerleader after the junior varsity game last night. I better go try to calm her down."

"Good luck," Jules said as she headed out of the dark hallway towards the classroom where the students were still eating.

On her way, she almost collided with Emily, startling them both. Jules was glad to see a familiar face, although she had been half looking for Miles. *Where was he?* Jules understood he needed space, but they couldn't avoid each other forever. A dull ache constricted in her chest hard to ignore.

"Ahh, you're here. Good," Emily said. "How's Winnie? Has she leveled out yet?"

"She seems to be just fine now, excited. Was she still anxious earlier?"

"A bit, but we received good news from the doctor earlier today, so I think that might have eased some of it," Emily shared, causing Jules to break into a big smile.

"I'm so happy to hear that, Emily. I know you two are going to be the best parents." It was true, Jules knew their baby would be so loved and cared for.

"And you'll be the best aunt ever," Emily added, filling Jules with an emotion she'd never experienced before. Warmth spread through her as she imagined herself holding their tiny sleeping baby swaddled in a blanket. She felt such an intense love for this child already; how could she go back to D.C. and miss everything? Winnie was the closest thing she had to a sister, so the thought alone was like another nail in the coffin of her writing dream.

After a few minutes, the lights flickered, signaling that it was time for the audience to take their seats; the show was about to begin. Jules had lost Emily in the shuffle to get to the theater, so she made her way down the center aisle alone to find a seat in the middle among the students and parents.

A few rows in front of her to the right, she spotted the back of a familiar head of wavy brown hair. It was Miles. Her heart skipped a beat at the recognition, but it quickly slowed when she noticed a woman sitting next to him. Jules didn't recognize her. The woman looked young, but not young enough to be a student.

Her auburn hair skimmed Miles' shoulder in a familiar way as they continued their animated conversation, punctuated with laughter and hand gestures. She couldn't make out any facial features with the angle and lighting, but it looked like they were enjoying each other's company.

Maybe she was a colleague? Another teacher? *It doesn't matter*, she told herself. Miles was an adult; surely, he had other female friends and acquaintances. But Jules couldn't stop wondering if the woman was his date. Her heart sank at the thought, and she stood up to move seats. Unfortunately, just then, the lights dimmed, and the curtains rose on stage. She sat back down. It would be a long show.

At intermission, Jules hurried out one of the back doors, eager not to run into Miles and his…friend. Luckily, she found another seat far away from the couple for the latter half of the show.

On stage, the students were giving it their all. The set props also looked like they'd undergone a facelift since she'd last seen it, making the production seem more professional.

The entire audience sat raptured until the last scene. After the curtain rose, the cast received a standing ovation and Winnie beamed on stage alongside them, bowing. All her work had paid off. Jules couldn't wait until tomorrow when they could celebrate together in Chicago.

As the audience made their way out of the theater and into the lobby where the cast members waited for their families, Jules looked around for Winnie and Emily. After an initial scan, she caught sight of them on a set of stairs holding court for a group of parents and students who shared their congratulations.

Her friends looked right at home, glowing with pride and love for each other. Jules watched as Emily wrapped her arm around Winnie's waist, who placed a hand on Emily's belly.

Their eyes said it all: they were in love and building a life together.

While she continued to admire them and the community of support that had turned out, underneath a seed of guilt began to take root, threatening to suck the life out of the joy she felt in that moment. Jules could feel the darkness and jealousy creeping into her conscious thought: Would she ever find a relationship like this? Did she deserve someone who loved her the way Emily loved Winnie? Why did she continue to sabotage herself every chance she got?

For just a moment, Jules let herself indulge before snapping out of it. This wasn't her night, it was Winnie's. And goddammit, she wasn't going to make this about herself.

Jules lifted her hand to give them a quick wave before turning around to head towards the door. It'd take forever to make her way up there through the crowd, plus she'd see Winnie tomorrow.

Turning to leave and throwing her jacket over her shoulders, her gaze caught on Miles pushing open the side door for the woman from earlier. For just a second, their eyes met, and Jules stood frozen to the floor, heart beating so loud she could feel it in her face. She held her breath, hoping he'd stop and come back to talk to her. Instead, he gave a barely perceptible nod and disappeared into the blackness of the night.

***

Winnie showed up almost twenty minutes late the next morning, but Jules couldn't be mad as her cute red VW Beetle crawled up the drive. She wondered if that was the real reason Winnie bought it, to ease the frustrations she caused by her terminal lateness. Either way, Jules couldn't contain her excitement to spend all day with Winnie in the city. It had been years since they'd last gone on an adventure together.

Cruising through town with the top down, they soaked up all the sun they could before fall set in. Although the city was just a quick forty-five-minute drive from Riverbend, it seemed a world away from the sleepy farm town. As they drove, the cornfields faded into the rearview mirror, giving way to crowded neighborhoods of townhouses lined with billboards for casinos and local radio stations.

First, they headed to Millennium Park to recreate a silly picture they had taken back in middle school with the park's famous "bean" sculpture. In it, Winnie crouched on all fours while Jules kneeled on her back, kissing the underside of the bean. They both still had a copy.

Now, however, it would be a test of their agility to recreate it, which they did before falling over in a heap of laughter. They didn't stay long, deciding to ditch the crowds of tourists and make their way to Wicker Park, where they'd spend the afternoon before dinner and the comedy show.

As they walked around the hip neighborhood, the sun reflected off the sidewalks and glass shop windows, casting the day in a bright glow that matched their moods.

Along the streets were dozens of independent shops that accompanied a few large brand names like Levi's and Urban Outfitters. Jules had never been a huge fan of shopping, but she had a soft spot for consignment and second-hand shops, which were aplenty here. They ducked in and out of various shops and art galleries throughout the neighborhood, enjoying the ease of being together. She had to remind herself to not go overboard on account of her current unemployment.

As the afternoon wore on, they split up when Winnie got lost in the massive Levi's store while Jules wandered down a quiet brick-laid backstreet. She was just getting ready to head back to the main road when she saw a weathered sign that read, "Spine & Spoon" hanging above a peeling green door tucked into the side of an old rowhouse.

Curious, Jules opened the door, which let out a pleasant jingle. A long, narrow room with floor-to-ceiling bookshelves on each wall stretched in front of her. Another handwritten sign at the back of the shop read, "Chicago's Only Cookbook Store."

Could it be that she found herself in a bookstore full of books about cooking? Who knew such a thing even existed?

Amazed, Jules started at the left side of the narrow room and worked her way around in a loop, gliding her hands over the spines of hundreds of cookbooks. At first, it seemed like a disorganized mess, but she realized the sections were grouped by topic. Everything from French and Italian cooking to books about famous chefs and restaurants to kitchen equipment manuals sat tucked in the shelves, waiting for someone to dust them off. This store had it all. Her earlier warning not to spend anything went out the window. At least a book or two would be coming home with her.

She texted Winnie to meet her there after she bought her denim. At one point, Jules sat on the floor in a bright corner, stacks of books around her as she held each one to her face, examining it; she wanted to read them all, but she had to be reasonable. She could only buy what she could carry, after all. These books were crafted out of passion and expertise, and Jules could feel the knowledge pulsing through the pages, alive and breathing in its own way.

After a while, she stumbled on a section of books about Italian food in Chicago throughout the nineteenth and twentieth centuries. One book was printed in all black and white and featured restaurants from the early to mid-nineteen-hundreds, complete with well-known recipes from each. Although it didn't mention her great-grandfather's restaurant, she knew Grandma Rosa would love it. She threw it on top of the pile that she'd designated as her "take-home" stack.

Deciding that was enough, she made her way to the register when the door jingled again and Winnie stepped through with a large shopping bag looped over her arm.

"Oh my, look at this place," she said, taking in the floor-to-ceiling bookshelves.

"Isn't it amazing? A bookstore just for cookbooks!" Jules almost squealed. The lady behind the counter smiled and said they got that reaction a lot.

Winnie grabbed a cookbook by Ina Garten and flipped through it, shuffling up to Jules to show her. Pointing at one page with a recipe for homemade pizza dough, Winnie said, "You know you could do this."

"Do what? Make pizza?" Jules asked, not paying attention. Of course she could make pizza.

"No, silly." Winnie slapped her shoulder. "You could write one of these."

Jules', now alert to what Winnie was saying, blew out a quick, "Me? No way! I don't know the first thing about writing cookbooks." Waiving Winnie off, Jules turned back to the lady waiting for her payment.

"No, Jules, I'm serious. You could really do this. You know how to write, you're an outstanding cook and you have your grandma to help you. I think you should consider it. Why not?"

"You're crazy," said Jules, although the thought seemed to already be worming its way into her brain. Maybe...she did have all those recipes just sitting at home.

All throughout dinner and then the show, Jules kept coming back to the conversation. She didn't know the first thing about writing a book, let alone a cookbook, but she could feel its allure. It would be the perfect marriage of creativity and skill. She loved to cook, and she was a decent writer, but how would she go about it? How did you even get a book deal these days; wasn't it hard? The questions kept bubbling up in her head as she laughed along to the improv actors on stage. Although the show was hilarious, her mind was elsewhere.

"That was a fun show. I think my abs are going to be sore tomorrow. I can't remember the last time I laughed that hard," Winnie said as they navigated their way back to the car. Jules agreed. Even though she'd only paid half attention, it was worth the drive.

"Thanks for coming today. I miss having adventures with you."

"I'd go to the ends of the earth for you, Jules. You know that," Winnie said, as they climbed into the clown-sized car. "Plus, I'm a sucker for dinner and show."

"Oh, don't I know it."

Making their way out of the dark city streets and back onto the highway, Jules asked Winnie what she thought she should do about Miles after recounting the last two conversations they'd had since she returned from D.C.

"Well, I can tell you've been thinking about him. You've avoided saying his name all day," she said with a heavy dose of side eye. "But I think you're asking the wrong question. You need to ask yourself what you really want, not what you think you should do because it's the sensible thing."

"What do you mean?" Jules tried to keep her tone light. She knew her best friend wasn't trying to hurt her feelings, but the comment felt like an accusation.

"You know what I mean. Jules, you've always been a hyper independent person, it's one of the many things I love about you. But you also use it as a shield. Ever since you and Miles broke up years ago, you've been afraid to let anyone else in. So instead, you've thrown yourself into being successful, building your career, and checking all the other boxes you can on your own."

Winnie took Jules' hand across the center console. "But you're not alone and you don't have to go through life alone. Now, don't get me wrong, I was never a huge fan of Luke. But you have to be honest, you had one foot out the door your entire relationship."

A lump formed in Jules' throat. She was quiet for a long minute before giving a silent nod. Winnie was right.

"If you're asking me, I think you already know in your heart what you want to do. You're just too afraid to admit it because then you'll have to give up a little control. You'll have to depend on others, and your future won't be certain."

"You mean I should write a cookbook?" Jules joked, attempting to divert the conversation.

"No. I mean, sure. If that's what you want. But what I'm talking about is letting go of your old life and embracing something new. Whatever you decide to do, whether it's going back to D.C. or staying in Riverbend, I think you deserve to find out what makes you happy and then do that. Because I know it's not writing for power-hungry white men who can't keep it in their pants," she said, cracking a smile.

Jules had to concede she had a point. It's possible that while she'd been trying to prove she could make it on her own, she inadvertently closed herself off to other possibilities, other versions of her life that would be just as fulfilling, if not more. But could she learn to trust more than just herself? History had taught her otherwise.

On one hand, Jules had learned the importance of self-reliance a young age, with her flighty mother and absent father to thank for that. But on the other hand, she'd been raised by one of the most fierce and loyal women she knew. It was because of Rosa and Grandpa Lou Jules even had the opportunity to dream of a better life. They'd sacrificed for her. Given so much of themselves to ensure she had a bright future. Jules always thought she owed it to them to do the expected thing: go to college, graduate, and get a safe, steady job. To dream even bigger was to risk it all.

But now, her thoughts slid into place. Maybe, just maybe, she owed it to her grandparents to do the risky thing. What if she'd been wrong this entire time? Didn't Grandma Rosa have her own dreams of owning a restaurant and being a chef when she was a young woman? She, too, likely thought that the reasons for not pursuing her dreams were valid. What if the best way to honor all her grandparents' work was to take a chance on herself?

The thoughts were too big for her tired brain to make sense of this late at night, so she resigned to deal with them tomorrow when she was functioning at full capacity again.

Tucked in her twin-sized bed, Jules read a text from Emily thanking her for taking Winnie out for the day. She said they'd both needed it. What Emily didn't realize was that Jules needed it just as much.

Surprisingly, Jules slept through the night and woke up with the sunrise, feeling refreshed and clear headed for the first time in days. Big decisions still loomed in the distance, but this morning they seemed less scary and more manageable.

Deciding to capitalize on her early start, Jules lugged a heavy bin of dirty clothes she'd been neglecting to wash to the basement washer and dryer. Doing laundry was the worst sort of chore in Jules' book. If she could never do another load again in her entire life, she'd die happy, but, alas, she was running out of clean clothes to wear.

She hadn't been down to the basement much since she'd been back, and it looked like her grandma didn't made it down too often, either.

The couch that had been there for decades still had a Christmas throw blanket hanging off one arm and the big box TV sitting on a rickety old stand had a thick layer of dust coating the top.

In high school, Jules would spend hours down here lying on the couch and watching reruns of Law & Order or talking on the house phone with Miles. To the left of the tidy living area was a large wooden door that was closed, concealing her grandpa's woodshop where he used to spend hours. She doubted anyone had been in there in the past two years.

Pushing the heavy door open, a cloud of dust filled her nostrils before she could reach in and flick the light switch on the wall. It still smelled the same: a mixture of earthy pine and sawdust that littered the floor. When she was around five or six, her grandfather took her down here for the first time and showed her the large tools he used. He explained how he used his table and jigsaw, showed her the dozens of chisels that hung on the wall over a large working desk and his old planer machine. He told her about how dangerous they could be but also showed her how they could help him turn a piece of wood into something special. Throughout the years, he often convinced her to help him work on whatever project he had going at the time. Between cooking with grandma Rosa and crafting something out of nothing with her grandpa Lou, Jules' love for creativity bore its way into her soul.

Jules looked around the cavernous room. Illuminated only by a single hanging light bulb and a tiny window, the morning rays caught on the dust specks floating in the air. Her eyes caught on the bottom stair of the concrete staircase that led to the outside of the house. An abandoned piece of wood was propped the corner. Jules picked it up, dusting it to reveal an engraving of loopy script in the corner. "For Rosa, my love," it read. It was one of Grandpa Lou's cutting boards. He loved to make them to give away as gifts, polishing the boards until they almost shone. This one looked dull, though, as if he hadn't finished it.

Jules knew just what to do. After finding some sandpaper and wax sealant, she polished the board, revealing the herringbone design he'd used in constructing it. It was a beautiful cutting board, fit for display in her grandma's kitchen.

Jules rushed upstairs to grab the book she bought as a gift last night and wrapped them both in silvery wrapping paper she found in the hallway closet. She hadn't planned to make such a fuss about the book, but now it seemed appropriate. Along with the wrapped gifts, Jules tucked a card under the ribbon she used to tie them together. The handwritten note simply thanked her grandma for being more than just a grandparent. She was her best friend, mentor, and mother all in one. The urge to ensure her grandma knew that felt urgent, like she couldn't wait another day. Jules didn't get the chance to thank her grandfather, and she would not make that mistake again.

Energy coursed through her veins as she sat back on the floor of her bedroom, admiring the gift set in front of her. She'd give it to her tonight after cooking a special meal for the two of them.

Jules got dressed and made her way back down to the kitchen. It was still early but she could hear Rosa stir upstairs. A low fog stretched across the front lawn as she looked out the window with a cup of tea warming her hands. She didn't need caffeine, feeling as awake as if she'd already had two shots of espresso. Grandma Rosa startled her as she came into the kitchen. "Are you going to answer that?"

Confused, Jules looked back with an eyebrow raised in question.

"Your phone is ringing," her grandma said, pointing to the table.

Chapter 17

Jules hadn't heard it at all. She'd been in her own little world and zoned it out. Now, though, she could hear it ringing and saw Miles' name flash across the screen. Jules picked it up.

"I'll give you some privacy," Grandma Rosa said, backing out of the room.

"Good morning?" Jules answered.

"Hi. Sorry to bother you so early. I hope I didn't wake you," Miles said in his morning voice that was so sexy a thrill swirled low in her belly. She did her best to ignore it. He'd only be calling this early if it were important.

"No, I've been up for a while."

"Oh. Good," he mumbled. "Well, Roxy asked me to call you. She went into labor last night—"

"What? Is she ok? Is the baby alright?"

"Yes, they are both great. Healthy little boy. They named him Oliver," Miles informed her. "But that's why I'm calling. She said you had volunteered to help her with the Bear Ball this week. She won't be able to do it now. So I had suggested that, um, maybe you'd be interested in taking over for her? I know it's a lot of work and you only have three days, but it would mean a lot to her, and I think you'd be great," he rambled on.

Jules' face scrunched in confusion. What was he asking her? To cook for the entire benefit? She'd never cooked for that many people, and never for an important event like this. When she volunteered to help, she expected Roxy to be there telling her what to do.

"Jules, you there?"

"Yeah, sorry. I'm just trying to get caught up. Is there no one else who'd be better at this?"

"No. I can't cook, you know that. And Jax is even more hopeless in the kitchen, if you can believe it," he explained. "They have a few high school kids scheduled to help, but no one who can take over. It would be a huge favor to them. And to me."

"Alright. Sure, why not? How hard can it be?"

She already felt in over her head.

Jules told Miles to get her all the information about the Bear Ball that he could. How many people would be there and had the food been ordered? Could he get the RSVPs so she could be prepared for allergies? There were so many details to sort out in just three short days; she needed reinforcements.

Jules rushed into the living room to get her grandma up to speed so they could decide what to serve for dinner. Roxy had a menu, but she didn't get the order placed in time for the fish she planned for the main course. The fresh haddock wouldn't arrive by Wednesday if they ordered it now; they needed a different plan.

Where to start, though? Jules flipped through the tin of organized recipe cards for inspiration. She was relieved to have her grandmother there to help. First, they worked to finalize a main dish they could build a cohesive menu around, which seemed like the hardest part. They'd also need a vegetarian plate based on the RSVP notes Jules now had in her email from Roxy.

As they discussed options, Grandma Rosa suggested chicken as the main protein because it would be easy to find in the quantity they needed for Wednesday and could be cooked in large batches. After considering a few recipes, they landed on roasted orange chicken thighs with artichoke and fennel. It was a hearty dish that had a lighter flavor profile, plus Jules had cooked it before.

They picked gnocchi alla sorrentina for the vegetarians, or non-vegetarians who preferred a pasta main. Her grandma cautioned her that people sometimes changed their minds the night of any preset dinner, so she should make extra.

For the appetizer, they went simple: a caprese salad. Dessert would be something Grandma Rosa could help Jules make ahead of time: strawberry honey mascarpone tart.

The menu focused on fresh ingredients and simple, yet beautiful presentation. This was not a time to overcomplicate things. They would just make good, satisfying food with the best ingredients they could get in time.

Satisfied with their selections, Jules thanked her grandma before stopping into the Golden Kernel. Roxy had emailed some instructions for Jules and had told her where to find a list of purveyors in the kitchen office that she should call to order whatever she needed. Knowing there was a possibility they might be able to get her everything in time, Jules thought she would start there and then head down to John's Shoppe if all else failed. Micky would know how to help.

The gastropub's kitchen wasn't much different from the one at The Landing, just smaller and more intimate. The tables and cooktops were well used but kept clean. The shelves were full and organized with supplies. Jules did a quick inventory of the equipment, pantry, and walk-in cooler so she'd be familiar when it came time to cook.

Her hands shook with adrenaline as she lifted various pots and pans to get a better look at the cook range. Everything seemed in order, but anxious energy coursed through her body. She didn't know if she could pull this off, and there was a lot of pressure to get it right. Roxy and Jax were counting on her. Miles was counting on her. The Golden Kernel was just starting to plant roots in Riverbend, but Jules had a sense it was still on shaky ground.

Before leaving the house earlier, Grandma Rosa gave Jules her version of a pep talk.

"Now don't go listening to those pesky voices in your head telling you that you can't do this. Of course you can. This isn't brain surgery. It's just cooking," she'd said. Oddly, it was just the right thing to calm her down. *This isn't brain surgery* was a familiar refrain to Jules; she'd often repeat it to herself in stressful situations, just as her grandma had advised her over the years. A reminder that nothing was as serious as it felt, unless it was brain surgery, of course.

Over the next few hours, Jules hunkered down in the office, making lists of everything she needed and placing orders over the phone. She was relieved to discover everything could be delivered in time except for the artichokes, which John's Shoppe carried. She'd never seen the store without them. Around her, the restaurant whirred to life for the lunch and dinner crowds, and without warning, Jax popped his mohawked head into the small office to say hello.

"You shouldn't be here!" she protested.

"Nah, it's all good. Roxy and the baby are taking a much-deserved nap, so I thought I'd stop by to talk to the staff. We have a few 'assistant managers' who will keep things running, but I have my doubts," he said with air quotes. "We're going to stick to the pared-down menu Roxy had arranged for her maternity leave. It'll be alright."

"Ok, well, if you need any help with things today, just let me know."

"You're already doing enough for the benefit. Thank you so much for jumping in with such little notice. You're a lifesaver. I can see why Miles loves you," he said before disappearing back into the dark hallway.

Jules' breath caught in her throat. The comment took her by surprise, leaving her frozen, staring at the beige bulletin board on the wall in front of her. *Had Miles told Jax he loved her? What did he mean? Did he mean it like a 'friend'? Was it an offhand comment, or was it more than that?*

Shaking herself back to reality, she lifted her shoulders and placed her hands in her lap, preparing for the serious talk she was about to have with herself. Out loud, she said, "All that matters right now is getting through the benefit. You have zero time to waste thinking about anything else for the next three days. Now focus, Jules. Worry later."

With the stern self-talk over, Jules looked at her to-do list. It was long.

Later, on her way to John's Shoppe, she called Winnie to enlist her help for Wednesday night. Although Roxy had already booked a staff for the Bear Ball, Jules knew she'd want a few familiar faces in the trenches. Of course, Miles would be there, but given their current situation, she doubted that would be much of a comfort. She was already battling the urge to interrogate Winnie about the woman Miles had brought to the play the other night. It took a mountain of strength to not bring it up yesterday.

At the promise of a free meal and the chance to witness the benefit in person, Winnie jumped at the opportunity to support Jules. Emily would join, too. The Bear Ball was known as the most exclusive event in town. Its invitee list included only

Riverbend's top influential and wealthy families, so being able to attend, even as staff, was exciting.

Jules spent the rest of the afternoon drafting a schedule for the next three days, along with going over the attendee list and run of show for the event. In total, more than one hundred people had RSVPed yes, including Mayor Maria Billingsworth and guest of honor Governor Matt Kash, who grew up in Riverbend. According to Roxy, it was the largest benefit dinner in the school district's forty-year history. The pressure kept mounting, but now that Jules had a plan, she felt more motivated than anxious. Her determination propelled her forward. She didn't want to slow down.

Jules emailed Benjamin from *WaPo* to postpone her follow-up call with the editor until Thursday after the dinner. Her faculties needed to remain focused. In all of the chaos, Jules had forgotten about the special dinner she'd planned to make for her grandma that evening until she was lying in bed, spent. Disappointed in herself, she made a silent promise to do it later that week, when she could give it her undivided attention.

As Monday morning rolled around, Jules worried she'd bit off more than she could chew with the benefit and her commitment to cook dinner at The Landing. Not wanting to let the ladies down, she tried to use their dinner as a test run for the benefit dinner on Wednesday. Rosa and Jules went to retirement village early together that afternoon to work out the recipe, perfecting it. With everything happening so fast, it was nice to slow down and focus on one task.

All of the excitement of the past few days kept her mind and body busy, leaving little time to think about the looming decisions she'd need to make soon about her future. Avoidance was a skill you didn't need until you needed it, and Jules was now becoming a master. She didn't care if it were a slippery slope to disarray, it was helping her in this moment. If she couldn't control her future, she sure as hell would control this benefit dinner.

The world and all its noise faded as Jules and Grandma Rosa worked for hours in the kitchen at The Landing, cooking test batch after test batch of the roasted chicken and gnocchi until they felt confident Jules could pull it off in her sleep. It took a few earnest tries to get the timing right on the roast and the perfect consistency for the potato gnocchi to sit well in the sauce, but the dishes were simple yet beautiful when they came together.

"I only wish I could see their faces when those fancy people taste what you've made," Rosa said as they sent out the last dinner plates at The Landing that evening.

They'd talked about Grandma Rosa helping Wednesday, but both agreed it would be too much for her. While she could get around plenty fine on her own now, she still had a hard time standing for long periods and needed frequent breaks. It was enough that she'd be helping prepare the desserts on Tuesday, which was a lot of work on its own.

The next few days seemed to be on fast-forward as Jules and Rosa did all they could to be ready for Wednesday night. They made the desserts, prepped as many of the ingredients as they could, and confirmed every detail of the service with the staff and Roxy via telephone.

Jules didn't hear at all from Miles, and her thoughts ran away with questions in her rare few minutes alone.

Was he thinking about her? Or was he with that other woman? And would she be able to act 'normal' around him on Wednesday?

Each time she caught herself in this familiar loop, she only had to glance at the never-ending to-do list to jolt her back to awareness. Her inner monologue played tug-of-war all day long.

Tuesday evening, Jax came back around to check on things. Jules seized the opportunity to ask him a question that had been lingering all day during a quiet moment in the office, "Umm, Jax, I know the attendee list for the benefit is set, but...do you think it would be possible to invite my grandma as a guest? She's been helping me so much the past few days, and I know it'd mean a lot to her."

Without a moment's hesitation, he replied, "It'd be an honor. Tell you what, I'll print out an official invitation for you to give to her. I can't wait to meet her."

Jules' heart swelled with joy. Grandma Rosa had never attended the Bear Ball, but Jules knew she'd always wanted to, even if she wouldn't admit it.

That evening, neither of them could muster the energy to cook much more than macaroni and cheese from a box. As they ate, Jules took the invitation Jax had given her from her purse and slid it over to her grandma.

"I know you won't be in the kitchen tomorrow, but I was hoping you'd come as a guest instead?" she asked. "You've done so much to help. You deserve to be there."

Grandma Rosa picked up the invitation, reading it over.

"You know, your grandpa always wanted to go to one of these," she said in a quiet voice.

Jules chuckled to herself. She knew that was code for, "I've always wanted to go to one of these."

"I think I might just have the perfect dress."

"You'll look beautiful in whatever you decide to wear. I'm glad you'll be there. Just knowing you're close will help keep me calm."

"Oh, honey, you don't need me for that. Look at everything you've done on your own. I'm so proud of you," she said, grabbing Jules' wrist. As Jules' eyes welled up, she knew it was time for bed.

"Thanks, Grandma, but I couldn't have done anything without you," she said, picking up their bowls to rinse in the sink. They both knew it was true. But as Jules laid in bed that night, she couldn't shake a sinking feeling in her gut.

Chapter 18

"No, I said it goes over there!" Jules heard someone yell to the back of the restaurant as she popped her head out of the office to see how the decorating was progressing the next morning.

The staff of volunteers and a few event managers brought in tables, chairs, linens, and a stage for the Bear Ball and had already been at work for hours transforming the place from a local pub to gala-worthy ballroom.

Jules didn't even recognize the place. There were dozens of round tables covered with cream linen and adorned with the most tasteful white, peach, and green floral and candle centerpieces. Dotted along them were gold chairs with large cream silk ribbons draped over the backs. Above, delicate twinkle lights swooped down from copper wire, giving the place an ethereal quality. The stage was positioned in front of the tables, stretched almost to the entire length of the wall. You wouldn't know you were standing in a pub unless you glanced at the deer and elk heads mounted over the bar area that could not be removed. A frenzied energy pulsed through the space as dozens of workers milled about, busy sorting out the details.

The day had started early for everyone. Jules had arrived just before six in the morning with the decorating crew, eager to receive the fresh food deliveries. As afternoon approached, even more people arrived, filling the space. Now, standing at the front of the restaurant, Jules took a quick break to admire the changes and greet Winnie and Emily.

"Thanks, again, for coming," Jules said as they made their way through the front door.

"Geez. This is something," Emily said, looking around. "Where do you want us?"

Apparently, two of the scheduled hostesses did not show up, so Jules directed Emily and Winnie to the front-of-house manager to help organize the registration table. It was going to be an all-hands-on-deck kind of evening.

Jules hurried back to the kitchen to continue prepping for dinner service. An hour later, she heard someone yell her name in the dining room, sending a flare of annoyance through her as she furiously chopped fennel. Setting her knife down, she wiped her hands on the chef's apron tied around her waist and strode out of the kitchen. As she rounded the entrance to the dining room, Jules saw Barb standing near the bar.

"Mom! What are you doing here?" Jules asked, surprised to see her.

"Someone said you might need some extra hands." Barb, leaned in for a hug. "Thought I'd stop by so you could put me to work." Her smile beamed at Jules.

"Who called you? I'm glad you're here, just a little confused." Jules pulled back to look at her.

"Your grandma called this morning."

"Oh, wow. That's...great," Jules stuttered, stunned yet elated that the two might be on the road to patching things up. It felt strange to have Barb here. Her entire childhood, Jules wanted Barb to be more like the reliable and doting mothers she saw from a distance at school, but that never happened. Now, decades later, her mom wanted to catch up. Better late than never, Jules supposed.

Jules walked Barb to the registration desk, where Winnie stood over a large stack of name tags. Winnie threw Jules an alarmed look. She was well aware of their strained relationship. But Jules just smiled and shrugged her shoulders. It didn't matter; she was just happy to have her people here.

Soon, it was go-time in the kitchen. Gathering everyone, Jules did a quick roll call, going over the detailed schedule she'd laid out last night.

"It's not brain surgery," she reminded herself and the entire staff, who were eager and dressed in their kitchen whites or professional-looking black staff uniforms. Jules had always dreamed of being a real chef. Now she felt like one.

As the kitchen staff worked to assemble appetizers and put the chickens in the large ovens to roast, a low buzz started in the dining room. Jules poked her head out to see dozens of people dressed in formal wear zigzagging through the tables looking for their seats. The line to the bar was already long enough to wrap around itself.

As she scanned the room, she caught a glimpse of Grandma Rosa making her way to a table with Barb at her side. She looked regal, dressed in a beautiful floor-length gown in a deep purple color fit for a queen.

Soft music could also be heard from the large stage where Miles was playing. He looked dapper in his grey suit and pale pink shirt with his hair combed back. Jules had forgotten how nicely he cleaned up. He wasn't alone though. Behind him was a serious-looking man playing the bass and a woman on saxophone—the same woman from the night of the play. The jazz song floated over the room with the ease of a band who'd been playing together for decades. Strangely, seeing the trio together on stage calmed Jules' suspicions from earlier. They might have only been colleagues after all.

Moments later, a voice came over the microphone, "Welcome, everyone, to this year's Bear Ball." Applause followed as someone on stage gave brief remarks and announced the first course being served.

Jules threw her hair up in a high ponytail as sweat rolled down her back, readying herself for the most stressful part of the evening as the kitchen worked to prepare the main course. Her body stretched in all directions as she tried to keep the train on the tracks while putting the finishing touches on each dish as it appeared on the expediting table. Her grandma had been right:

fifteen people changed their main dish selections upon checking in at the registration table. Thankfully, she'd planned for that.

As soon as the main course went out, Jules checked in with the crew handling dessert. It was all coming together, and they were now in the home stretch. Jules' adrenaline continued to pull her along as she handed the finished plates off to the servers. The entire process felt like a well-oiled machine, humming along to an invisible metronome, the sinking feeling from last night nowhere to be found.

Soon enough, the attendees finished the main course and were looking forward to dessert. The small square white plates topped with tarts full of sliced strawberries and mascarpone had been assembled earlier, but the garnishes needed to be placed. A team of three chefs surrounded a low metal table in the middle of the kitchen, holding metal tweezers as they placed the mint leaves and micro edible flowers atop the minitarts, setting them aside in a line to be served—all 120 of them. Jules had a few extras, just in case.

With dessert on its way out, she had a moment to breathe. The hard part was over, and they'd avoided any catastrophes. Her limbs felt heavy with overuse, but her heart was full.

She did it, with a lot of help.

After a while, Emily and Winnie found their back to the kitchen, doling out high fives. They said the guests were raving about the food. Everyone seemed satisfied and full and were now filling the dance floor as they finished their desserts. For the kitchen staff, the night was winding down. Jules took a moment to look around and realized she hadn't seen her mom since before the service began.

Turning to Winnie, she asked, "Do you know where Barb is?"

"That's a good question. I saw her a few minutes ago talking to your grandma by a table."

As if on cue, Barb dashed through the swinging kitchen door with a crazed look on her face.

"Where's Jules?" she shouted, stopping mid-stride when she spotted Jules standing next to Winnie.

"What's wrong?" Jules asked, scared but a little skeptical.

"Grandma, she slipped. We need to call an ambulance."

Jules heart sank. "What? Where is she?"

"In the bathroom. She slipped on a puddle, I think."

"Winnie, call 911," Jules shouted over her shoulder, pushing through the door.

They both ran across the dining room and behind the stage to the restroom. Sure enough, her grandma was lying on the floor next to the sink, moaning and grabbing her hip.

"Oh my God, Grandma! What happened?" Jules asked, falling on her knees next to her grandma.

"Oh, I think I fell on the new hip. Silly me, I was starting to get used to it," Rosa said in a weak voice.

"I should have gone with you, Mom. I'm sorry," Barb murmured. Rosa shushed her, patting her hand.

Winnie cracked the door to say an ambulance was on its way. The next few minutes were a blur. Fortunately, there was a back exit next to the restrooms, so Grandma Rosa was spared the embarrassment of being pushed through the crowd on a stretcher. The other guests didn't even notice, caught up in dancing and conversation.

Winnie and Emily drove Jules and Barb to the hospital, following the ambulance. The two Cuccia women held hands in the backseat, not saying a word, but thinking about all the ways they could have prevented this.

Once in the emergency room, there wasn't much anyone could do but wait for news from the doctor. They took their seats in the cold, empty waiting room. Jules insisted Winnie and Emily go home and get some rest and promised to keep them updated. Although Jules' body felt the full day of hard work, she couldn't sit still.

"How do you know she slipped on water?" she asked Barb, who sat slumped in an uncomfortable wood and vinyl chair.

"I don't. I guess I just assumed she slipped. She fell somehow, though."

"We'll know more soon, hopefully," Jules responded, her stomach growling in protest. "I'm going to find a vending machine. Want anything?"

"No, thanks. I'm too wound up to eat."

"Fair enough." Having her mom there made Jules less nervous, but she still wanted answers about what happened and sitting around would not get her any closer.

As she approached the information desk to ask for directions, the automatic doors to her right slid open in her peripheral vision. Distracted and running on fumes, she rounded the corner of the desk and walked right into someone. Her vision was slightly blurred from exhaustion and hunger, but she knew who it was.

Miles wrapped his arms around her upper shoulders, so her head rested on his chest that smelled like it always had, sweet and musky.

Warmth spread down her arms and over her front. Their bodies melted together, oblivious to the situation. Gaining her composure, Jules craned her neck to look up at him without stepping from his embrace.

"Hi. You're here."

"I'm here. Are you alright? How is your grandma?" he asked, looking down at her, worry stretched across his face.

"I'm fine. We're fine, I guess." Jules looked over her shoulder at her mom who was still sitting in the waiting room. "We don't know what's happening with my grandma yet. Still waiting to hear from the doctors."

"That makes sense. Are you ok with Barb being here?" He cocked an eyebrow.

"Yes, she came to the benefit tonight to help. My grandma called her." Two nurses pushed past them in the narrow corridor, forcing them to separate.

"I was just going to grab some dinner from the vending machines."

"How very gourmet of you, Chef," Miles responded with a playful grin.

Jules both loved and hated how he could make her heart race even in a hospital emergency room waiting area. Being here showed he cared, right? Although any decent friend would do the same thing, so it likely didn't mean any more than that. Afterall, she was the one who'd poured cold water over their fling. What a mess she'd made of her own feelings.

Miles followed her down the bright hallway and helped her pick out a variety of junk food to bring back.

"Mind if I stay to keep you company?" he asked.

"Sure, but distract me. Tell me all about the rest of the night." Jules led him back to the waiting area, where Barb gave him a tentative hug and thanked him for coming.

"The benefit was wonderful. Everyone I talked to was raving about the food and the entire evening."

"I hope we didn't ruin the vibe."

"Not at all. I don't think anyone even noticed. They were too busy socializing and dancing. Plus, many of them were already a few drinks in to pay attention to anything but themselves. But don't worry about that. It's not important."

"Who were you playing with on stage?" Jules couldn't help herself. She needed to know.

"Oh, they're my friends from college. I played at their wedding, so they owed me a favor. They came down from Michigan for a few days to spend some time here and visit Chicago," he explained. "Ryan had a gig in Chicago on Friday, so his wife Justene came with me to the play."

That made sense. It also made Jules feel so much better.

Just then, her phone dinged with a message from Roxy.

> *First, how is your grandma? I hope she's ok. Next, THANK YOU! You rocked it tonight. Dare I say it was even better than what I had planned? I owe you big time.*

A picture of Oliver was attached, looking milk drunk and as cute as a button. Jules leaned over to show Miles, who smiled and nodded as he slipped his hand around hers. Jules felt like her heart could explode out of her body at any moment. She wasn't used to this rollercoaster ride of emotions. The night had not gone as planned, but she was so grateful not to be alone in this moment.

Looking across at her mom, Jules saw the worry etched onto her face. It had been years since Jules had truly looked at Barb. Whenever she'd pictured her mom, an image of the young thirty-something-year-old from her childhood days flashed in her mind. Now, age swept across her mother's features, changing the once youthful woman into a more refined version of herself. Coupled with her shoulder-length brown hair streaked with strands of light grey, her mother finally resembled what Jules had always thought a mom should look like. How long had Barb been this unfamiliar woman? How had Jules not noticed? Shame rushed through her. She wanted to know *this* Barbara. The woman who was working hard to better her life and be there for her family. Jules had punished her long enough; it was time to forgive and move forward.

After what seemed like an eternity, a middle-aged Black woman wearing light blue scrubs and a stethoscope came through the hallway, asking for Rosa Cuccia's family. They hurried to gather around her.

"Hi, I'm Doctor Sampson. Your mom is doing fine," she said to Barbara. "But I will need to keep her overnight for observation. We think she might have had a dizzy spell from the medication she's on, causing her to fall. We need to monitor things before she can go back home."

"Thank you, Doctor," Barb said, nodding her head.

"What about her hip? Is it alright?" Jules cut in.

"Yes, it's fine, thankfully. She'll have a nasty bruise, but nothing is broken. She'll be ready for visitors soon. I'll have a nurse come get you."

They thanked the doctor again, feeling lighter now.

"I'll stay here tonight," Barb said. "I don't want her to be alone."

Surprise flashed across Jules' face. For once, Jules didn't have to be the responsible one. It comforted her to know Barb would be there for her grandma, and she appreciated her mom's concern. It would have been easy for Barb to turn her back on Rosa after she'd been iced out for over a year. Jules hoped time alone together would help them both heal.

Soon, a nurse led them to her grandma's room where she lay propped up in a hospital bed, lights low. It was getting late, but the nurse said they could see her for a few minutes, even though visiting hours were over.

"Hi, Grandma," Jules said as she sat next to the bed. "How are you feeling?"

"Like a million bucks. I think I'll sign up to run the Chicago Marathon this year," she joked in a quiet voice. They all chuckled, glad to know her grandma hadn't lost her sense of humor. "Nice to see you here, too, Miles."

Rosa told them she wasn't sure what happened in the bathroom. One minute she was washing her hands in the sink, and the next she was waking up on the cold, damp floor, disoriented. No one even entered the bathroom until a few minutes later, when Barb had gone to find her.

"Thank you, Barb, for checking on me. I would have died on the spot if someone like the mayor had found me," her grandma admitted in her own sincere way. "Speaking of the mayor, what a night you all pulled off! It was wonderful. And the food, absolute perfection! Now, you'll have to come back every year to cater the event."

Miles' eyes flicked to Jules. His face was full of shadows, but she thought she saw a hint of a question: *had she decided to go back to D.C. and didn't tell him*? She shook her head to calm his unspoken fear. Right then, in the dark hospital room, surrounded by her family and the man she'd never gotten over, Jules knew what she wanted. If only she could tell him the truth about what happened all those years ago.

"Barb, Miles, sweet dears, can I have a moment alone with Jules?" her grandma asked.

What did her grandma need to say to Jules that she couldn't say in front of these two?

After a moment of awkward silence, Miles and Barb both rose from their chairs and excused themselves into the hallway.

Chapter 19

Once they were alone, Jules scooted her chair closer to her grandma's bed.

"What is it?" she asked, holding her hand that felt like soft tissue paper.

"You don't know the entire truth about what happened all those years ago on your prom night and you should—" Rosa began.

"I know enough, Grandma," Jules said, shifting in her seat.

"No, you don't. I'd hoped that Miles would tell you someday, but I don't think he will." She took a deep breath in and continued, "Your grandfather was police commissioner back then and heard what really happened from the patrol officers on duty." She paused. "Miles did indeed get arrested for stealing a car with his cousin...I forgot his name, but the one who was always getting himself into trouble."

"Ricky," said Jules.

"Yes, that's the one. As you know, the boys crashed the car into a ditch near the community center that night. Officers were called to the scene by someone who'd witnessed it. That's how they were caught." Jules knew this much. She'd hated Ricky for getting Miles tangled up in his illegal activity.

"By the time they'd arrived, both boys were standing outside of the car, so they couldn't tell who was actually driving. But Ricky was intoxicated." She looked at Jules with hooded eyes, trying to convey a point that Jules wasn't understanding. Everyone knew Miles was driving. That's why he went to jail; it's the reason his life spun out of control for so many years. Jules never understood why, though.

"Jules, honey, they didn't think Miles was driving. They thought it was the other boy. That he had picked Miles up in the stolen car and crashed it because he was drunk. Turns out, his cousin had a warrant, so this would have sent him to jail for a very long time. And Miles knew that. The police tried to get them to tell the truth, but they both stuck to the story that Miles stole the car and swerved to avoid hitting a deer."

Jules had tried for years to block that night out. After Miles didn't come to pick her up for their senior prom like planned, she called him furiously for hours until the calls went straight to voicemail. Jules assumed he'd turned his phone off. She spent the evening watching old movies with her grandma, fighting back tears. It wasn't until the next morning that she'd been told what happened: Miles had been arrested for stealing a car from the parking lot of a convenience store and was being held in county jail.

At first, Jules didn't believe it. He'd never do that. Not Miles. He knew what was at stake. He had a full ride scholarship, for

God's sake. She waited for him to call and sort everything out. It had to be a mix-up. But day after day, her phone went silent. Not so much as a text from him. Eventually, doubt crept in. It didn't help rumors were swirling the next week at school.

A few days later, Jules cracked. Her anger at him standing her up subsided, turning into worry. When she asked Grandpa Lou to help her get in touch with him at the county jail, he said Miles had already been released. That's when it became clear: he didn't want to talk to her. If he did, he would have called when he got out to set things straight and apologize or at the very least show up to school to talk to her.

Her concern turned back into hurt and furry, wondering how he could so easily walk away when she needed him more than ever. Soon, the pain morphed into indignation.

If he didn't need her, she didn't need him, she'd told herself. A few weeks later, she left Riverbend, skipping their graduation ceremony, to move with her mom to Lincoln, Nebraska. Barb had a boyfriend there who was working as a farmhand on a large soybean farm and the job came with a rustic hunting cabin. To her eighteen-year-old brain, it was the perfect solution for Jules since she'd be attending school there in the fall, anyways.

After Grandma Rosa finished telling Jules the truth about that night, they were told visiting time was over, but they could come back tomorrow when she was being discharged at noon. Hugs were given all around and Jules told Barb to call if she needed anything at all.

Still processing what her grandma had told her, she followed Miles to the large and almost empty parking lot, stopping abruptly at the edge of the sidewalk.

"Um, I don't have a car," she said, looking around in a daze, her mind elsewhere.

How could he have not told her? Why did he push her away? Was he trying to protect her?

"Don't worry. I've got you," he said, taking her hand again and leading her to his white pick-up truck that was still full of his gear from playing at the dinner earlier.

Jules let him take the lead, feeling a mixture of comfort at his touch but also revulsion at herself for believing the worst about him. Of course, he wasn't the one driving. Of course, he wanted to protect her by keeping her as far away from his problems as possible. She was angry with herself for not fighting hard enough for him.

Lost in her thoughts, she kept quiet as the truck hugged the dark, curving back roads from the hospital to her grandma's neighborhood. After a few minutes, Miles pulled over to the side of the road.

"What are you doing?" she asked.

"I don't think you should stay by yourself tonight," he said, holding his palms up to let him continue. "Hear me out. You've had a long, stressful day that ended with an emergency. I think you should stay at my place so you're not alone." He stared at her with one hand on the wheel and the other reaching across the dash to squeeze her shoulder.

She cocked her head to the side, suspicious but also touched he cared that much. Could she trust herself to be with him right now? Wasn't there too much to process?

"You can have the bed. I'll sleep on the couch. Tomorrow is a school improvement day, so I don't have to be there until the afternoon. I can drop you back at the Golden Kernel to pick up your grandma's car," he explained.

Miles was right; Jules didn't want to be alone tonight. So, against her better judgment, she agreed, and Miles threw the truck in reverse, turning around to drive towards his house before she could change her mind.

The familiar house was dark and motionless as they drove up, but it still gave Jules the same cozy feeling as they crossed the threshold of the front door. Sir-Toots-A-Lot was doing figure eights around her legs before she could even get her shoes off.

"I think someone missed you," Miles said as he hung their jackets on the hand-made hall tree by the front door. Jules bent down to run her fingers through the cat's thick fur, and he purred in return. "Come on, let's get you some pajamas."

Miles made his way towards the bedroom hallway as she followed behind. Her body was on the brink of giving out, but her mind was awake and firing questions all over the place. Should she talk to him about what her grandma told her? Did it matter now?

No, she didn't need to talk to him about it. *And yes*, it did matter. It was all so clear to her now, watching him lay out one of his t-shirts and a pair of boxers on the bed for her. He'd never do anything he thought would harm her. He'd always taken care of her. Even back then, although misguided.

Standing in his room, she could see it all and ached to feel connected to him again. Jules took a confident step towards Miles, who had his back to her as he closed the drawer on his large wooden dresser. He turned to face her as she grazed his neck with her fingertips.

"Jules," he breathed into the space between them.

"I need to be honest with you," she said in return, meeting his gaze. She wouldn't give in to her need to feel his body against hers before he knew the whole truth about the darkness she'd been carrying since that summer. Miles deserved to know, even though it terrified her. He may never speak to her again after this, and she wouldn't blame him. But she knew his secret now, so it was only fair he knew hers, too.

Miles could sense the seriousness in her voice. "Let's go sit on the couch."

Jules shook her head yes and walked back down the dark hall, dread forming a heavy pit in her stomach.

"What is it, Jules?" Miles face was contorted with concern.

Jules was about to hurt him, again. She hated herself for it.

"I need to be honest with you about what happened the summer after we graduated, and you might not look at me the same after," she started.

Miles tilted his head to the side and narrowed his eyes as if to say, *What do you mean?*

"Instead of going to our graduation ceremony, I left for Nebraska to live with my mom," she continued.

"Yeah, I think I knew that. You left because of me. I'm so sorry I messed everything up." She held up a hand to stop him.

"You don't have to explain. I know why you did what you did. Just please listen. You're not the only reason I left for Nebraska early." Jules looked down at her hands clasped in her lap. It was hard to look him in the eyes. How could she say this out loud? She hadn't talked about it since that summer, trying to put it all behind her. Now, though, sitting across from Miles, the old pain welled up, threatening to consume her again.

Taking a few steadying breaths, she forced herself to say it. It had to be done.

"I went because I was pregnant," she whispered, lowering her chin but still watching for his reaction. Miles' entire body went rigid, and he sat up ramrod straight, a puzzled look on his face. "I found out the morning of prom and was planning to tell you, but then, you know...so, I decided moving away would give me time to figure out what to do."

Jules took in a long, steadying breath, stealing herself for the worst part. The part that still haunted her dreams and kept her from having any meaningful relationships since.

"But it turns out, I didn't have to decide anything. I lost the baby a few weeks after."

For a long moment, Miles said nothing.

"I understand if you're upset. But back then, I thought you didn't want to be with me. That your silence was a way of telling me you didn't care," she said, feeling relieved it was now out in the open but still terrified she'd lose him all over again. "But now I know differently. I'm so sorry for not telling you, Miles."

This time, she met his stare, trying to convey the depth of her regret through her eyes.

Miles looked down at the black and white striped rug tucked under the couch before closing the space between them and wrapping his arms around Jules in a deep hug. Jules could feel a tear escape down her cheek, but she didn't care. For a moment, they just held each other.

"You're so strong," he said into her neck. "I can't imagine how hard that was. Jesus, Jules, I'm so sorry you had to go through that alone."

"Do you hate me?"

"I could never hate you." They drew back to look at each other. "I have always loved you. I never stopped."

Jules felt as if she were weightless, like a vise had loosened and she could breathe again. Without thinking, she told him that she loved him, too. And she meant it. It'd always been Miles. They could never be friends because they were meant for so much more.

Miles brought his hand up her neck to clasp the back of her head as he guided her to his lap. His lips covered hers in a kiss so intense, it drew the breath out of her. His hunger burned as he ran his other hand under her shirt and up her back, greedy for more. It was as if they were eighteen again, before they had secrets and could freely love each other.

Finally, Jules found the missing ingredient she'd been searching for all these years. One that she still craved.

Jules wrapped her legs around his waist as he lifted her up and carried her to his bed, lips never leaving hers. In the room, he lowered Jules to the bed, straddling her on all fours as he looked down at her with a gaze so deep it bored into her soul. He expertly lifted her shirt and unclasped her bra, taking them both off over her head in one fluid motion. Jules watched as he leaned down, taking her breast in his hand and closing his mouth around her nipple. She let a soft moan escape before he trailed his tongue down to her belly button and lifted his head to look at her. His eyes were an intense shade of green she'd never seen before, but it made her ache for him even more, and she squirmed in excitement under his weight.

"Don't move," he growled, pinning his hands on either side of her hips as his mouth continued down her stomach until he reached the waist on her jeans, which he unbuttoned and slid down.

"I want to taste you," he whispered, lighting a blazing flame of heat low in her body. She wanted him—no, needed him more than ever. As he took her in his mouth, Jules wove her fingers through his hair and wrapped her legs around his upper back, lost in his touch.

Jules didn't notice him remove his pants, but she thanked God he did, because she was close to the edge of control with his face between her legs. Before she knew it, their eyes locked again, and he thrust deep inside her as they moved together in a rhythm that felt natural, like their bodies had known each other over lifetimes. Jules grasped his back, and they came together, his muscular arms gripping her.

That night, Jules slept like she'd never slept before, deep and secure.

The next morning, bright sunlight poured into Miles' bedroom through the row of windows behind his bed, waking them both. In their haste, they'd forgotten to close the curtains the night before. They rolled over to face each other, content but sleepy.

"Are you ok? Do you regret last night?" Jules asked. She knew it was too much to ask him to forgive her. He'd need time, of course, and she was willing to wait.

"No, I don't regret it at all. But I do have a question."

Jules froze.

"Will you stay in Riverbend?" he asked, a small smile brightening his face.

Chapter 20

Barb hung around Riverbend for a few more days to keep an extra set of eyes on Rosa. The doctor said she'd be fine. Two of her medications had interacted poorly, causing the light-headedness, which she'd apparently been experiencing for weeks. Barb and Jules both made Rosa promise to tell them if she was ever having any side effects again and she begrudgingly agreed.

In the commotion of the past day, Jules had almost forgotten about the call she had scheduled with Julian from the *Washington Post*. Needing some air, she stepped out on the front porch to take the call, noting that the yard needed to be mowed.

As she sat on the concrete steps waiting for his call, Jules thought of the dream she had the previous night, wrapped in Miles' arms. In it, someone she didn't recognize handed her a large, heavy book. She could see it as clearly as if it were with her now: the book was simple, adorned with a red trim and cream background on the cover and a title in a handwritten script that read, "A Recipe Called Home." Her name stretched across the bottom in block letters.

When Jules' phone rang in her hand, she rolled her shoulders back and answered, "Hi, Julian. I think I know what I want to write now, but I need your help."

***

"You take the bedroom, Mom. I can sleep in the basement or on the couch in the living room for a few nights," Jules said to Barb over dinner that night.

"Or at Miles'," her grandma said with a devilish grin. Jules smacked her arm but didn't deny it. Miles would be a part of her life, one way or another.

For dinner, Jules had made a special seafood pasta and delectable tiramisu cake to make up for the special meal she'd planned for them last weekend that had to be postponed for Bear Ball preparations.

The three generations of women sat around the small kitchen table, just as they had hundreds of times before. It was special, that table. It served as a refuge in the storm, a place of celebration and sometimes mourning. It had been witness to their lives. But right now, the table connected them.

Jules got up to clear their dinner plates, but instead of bringing the cake to the table, she set down a set of wrapped gifts in front of Grandma Rosa.

"I've been waiting to give these to you," she said. Barb leaned forward to get a better view. Jules stopped her grandma as she reached for the card first. "Read that last."

Following instructions, she peeled the wrapping paper off at the taped seams of the larger package. Taking her time, she folded the paper into a neat pile next to her and examined the gift. She inhaled, sliding her fingers over the inscription her husband had carved into the heavy wooden cutting board in front of her.

"Oh, Jules. Where did you find this?" she asked.

"In Grandpa's workroom. He left it on the stairs, just waiting for someone to finish it."

"Thank you," she said, eyes locked on the board. "He must have left it for you to find. He knew I'd never step foot in that dusty place."

Jules loved the way her grandma's face softened when she talked about Grandpa Lou. They were still connected, even through space and time. She caressed the cutting board, placing it on the table and tapping it twice for good measure.

Next, she opened the second gift, which was smaller but just as heavy.

"What is it?" Barb asked.

"It's a cookbook I found when Winnie and I were in Chicago. I thought Grandma would enjoy it," Jules said. Turning back to her grandma, she added, "It highlights old Italian restaurants and recipes from the neighborhoods you'd be familiar with."

She thanked Jules, thumbing through it before setting it down next to the cutting board and lifting the flap on the card Jules had rewritten that afternoon, following her call with Julian. As she read, her eyes flicked up to her granddaughter in shock and delight. She tenderly folded the card back into its envelope and placed it with the other gifts.

"I knew you'd figure it out. And you know you can stay here as long as you like. It's your home, too."

"So does that mean you'll help me write it?"

"Write what?" her mom asked, as if she were missing out on a shared secret. They both laughed, each grabbing a hand around the table to form a circle.

"Our very own cookbook," Jules said.

<h1 style="text-align:center">Epilogue</h1>

May 2024

Jules took one last look at herself in the full-length mirror behind the bathroom door in her house—the one she now shared with Miles after breaking the lease on her D.C. apartment. She couldn't decide if she looked ridiculous or appropriately dressed for Riverbend High's senior prom. Her sleeveless red satin gown hugged her body, skimming the floor over her silver heels and the sharp V-shaped neckline complimented the soft waves in her hair, plunging to a conservative depth but stopping just before revealing too much for an adult chaperone.

Before she could second-guess her dress choice, Miles appeared behind her, placing a lingering kiss at the nape of her neck.

"You look stunning. I'll have to beat all those hormone-riddled teenage boys away with a stick."

Jules rolled her eyes, grateful he liked the dress. When Miles asked her to be his date as a chaperone to the prom, they both thought of it as a second chance, and she wanted to make the most of it.

Miles grabbed Jules' hand and spun her around to face him. He held out a white cardboard box for her to open. In it laid a simple corsage made with white roses and silver ribbon. It went perfectly with her dress. He slid it over her wrist and wrapped her arm around her waist so they could admire themselves together in their reflection. Jules loved when Miles dressed up, which didn't happen often. It reminded her of his many sides that she loved: casual, capable, and self-assured in paint-splattered jeans or a tux, as he wore today.

Grabbing her clutch off their bed, Jules followed Miles to the front door, stopping just before she left to take a selfie with Sir-Toots-A-Lot just before leaving, her sidekick in the months since she'd moved in.

At first, it felt strange living in a house he'd made his own, but it didn't take long for her to leave her mark. Now, it perfectly combined his masculine artist energy and her polished, pared down aesthetic; somehow it worked.

As they stepped out onto the wooden front porch, Miles shook his head, laughing. "Jules, not again."

"What? They needed another friend," she said, referring to three gnomes, which were only two yesterday, flanking the door. "Don't pretend you don't love it," she teased, bouncing down the steps to his car.

"Ok, but no more. That's enough now!" He raced after her, smiling.

They met Winnie and Emily at the entrance to the gymnasium, under an enormous banner that read, "Glitz and

Glam Galore in 2024." Three weeks earlier, Emily gave birth to a healthy baby girl, Emmerson, who was now being watched by Barb for their first night out alone.

"How's my precious goddaughter?" Jules asked, pulling Winnie, then Emily in for a hug.

"Oh, you know, just sleeping and pooping. Living the life," Emily said through a tired yet contented smile.

Once inside, the two couples kept to the edges of the dancefloor, eyes open for teens smuggling in booze or making out in the dark corners, although Jules wouldn't discipline any of them. Part of her still felt like the teenage Jules, giddy and nervous to see where the night would take her. Plus, she didn't work here; it wasn't her job.

As if the universe heard her thoughts, she felt her phone buzz in her clutch and stepped out the door into a bright hallway to take a call from Julian.

"Hi, Julian, sorry for the noise," she said, one finger plugging her other ear so she could hear him over the bumping base from the music.

"It's no problem at all. Sorry for bothering you this late on a Saturday, but I wanted to let you know we have a publisher for the book. They sent the signed contract over this afternoon," he shouted in her ear.

Over the past nine months, Jules had started writing a regular column for the *Washington Post* focused on home cooking. She interviewed chefs, professionals who enjoyed cooking, and even bloggers about the best recipes and ways for feeding yourself and your family when you also worked a full-time job. It was a nice hybrid of what Julian had asked Jules to write and her rediscovered passion.

As a part of the deal, Julian agreed to help find a publisher for the cookbook she pitched using her grandma's story and recipes.

"That's amazing news! Thanks for all your help, Julian, sincerely. I couldn't have done it without you."

"Yes, you could have. But I'm grateful to have a small part," he said before hanging up.

The night sped by until Jules and Miles got the sappy slow dance they never had years ago. He kissed her, whispered, 'I love you,' then dipped her with a playful flourish for the kids.

In that moment, Jules felt her teenage self finally heal—proof that the messy road had indeed led to something beautiful.

***

Every recipe has an origin story. Find Grandma Rosa's in *The Kitchen We Keep.*

Author Acknowledgements

This book would not have been possible without the unwavering support of my husband, Thomas, and encouragement from my son, Theodore. Thank you both for pushing me to pursue this life-long dream and keeping me fed and nourished along the way.

I'd also like to thank my friends and family who read many drafts of the book, scenes, and gave feedback on my cover design. Your thoughtful messages and critiques helped in more ways than you will ever know.

And finally, I'd like to thank Maria Secoy and the All Write Well group for their invaluable guidance and wisdom throughout the writing and publishing process. I don't know where I'd be without you, but it certainly wouldn't be here.

About the Author

Stephanie Nelson is a speechwriter, creative marketing consultant, and budding romance novelist. She holds a B.A. in Journalism and Political Science from the University of Iowa and studied Professional Writing and Rhetoric at George Mason University. She now resides in Fredericksburg, VA with her husband, son, and three dogs.

Connect with Me

Follow me on Instagram @AuthorStephanieNelson &

@Stephlovessbooks